MARY, MARY

D.L. SLETTEN

Mary, Mary

D. L. Sletten

ISBN–13: 978-1-941212-88-2

Cover Designer: Deborah Bradseth

Novels by D. L. Sletten

Where Has She Gone?

She Didn't Die

PROLOGUE

She stood at the top of the stairs, waiting for Abby's automatic stair-lift chair to make it all the way up. As usual, the older woman was complaining.

"You're so useless," Abby said, her voice scratchy from years of smoking. "You know I like to come upstairs and get in bed before six o'clock so I can watch *Wheel of Fortune* while I eat dinner."

"I'm sorry," she said. "It couldn't be helped. I can't always leave work on time."

"Well, I hope you're happy. I'm missing my show, and my dinner is late. Seems to me you could think about others once in a while. You're selfish, just like your father. He always hid downstairs in that damn basement and never helped with you kids. Never! Useless and selfish!"

She stood rigid, waiting for the chair. It moved so slow, it grated on her nerves. It was bad enough Abby was screaming at her, but she couldn't even walk away because she had to help Abby out of the chair and assist her to the bedroom.

"I'm doing the best I can," she said, trying desperately to

be patient.

"Your best isn't good enough!" Abby said. She started coughing, a reaction from her yelling. "You'll never be anything in this life. You'll always be a loser."

The chair ground to a halt at the top of the stairs. She bent down to unhook the safety belt from around the older woman's ample waist, but Abby slapped her away.

"I'm old, not incompetent," she yelled, coughing again.

She offered her hand to Abby to help her out of the chair. This was the tricky part. If Abby lost her balance getting out of the chair, she could easily fall down the stairs.

Reluctantly, Abby took her hand, and she pulled her up and out of the chair. Abby's weight was growing heavier by the week. Abby refused to eat healthy food. She liked her Pepsi, cigarettes, and chips, and she wouldn't give them up.

For a split second, she stood there grasping the older woman's hand and staring down the staircase. All she had to do was let go. That's it. And then the woman who has made her life hell for years would be out of her life.

Abby took a tentative step toward her and then released her hand. She looked her up and down. "And would it hurt you to dress nice for a change instead of so dumpy? Look at you in that baggy suit. No wonder your husband left you."

Anger flared inside of her. How dare this woman say such a nasty thing.

"Look at me, Mother," she said, glaring down at Abby. "Look me in the eyes."

The older woman stared up at her, and her face suddenly became pale and slack. "You. It's you! But how?"

As her lips curled into a smile, she lifted her hand and pushed.

CHAPTER ONE

Mary
Eight Months Later

Mary Westin rushed from her bedroom to the kitchen to grab coffee in a to-go cup. She was running late and needed to be at work on time today. She'd been asking for a promotion for nearly two years since passing her CPA test, and it wouldn't look good on her record if she were late even once.

Mary's phone buzzed as she poured coffee into her favorite Yeti tumbler, and she glanced at it. She sighed. Conrad again.

"I can't talk right now," she said, answering the phone. "I'm already running late."

Her ex-husband snorted. "You? Late? When have you ever been late for anything except for sending my check?"

"I've had a tough month, Conrad," she told him. "The washing machine died, and I had to replace it. I promise, I'll bring your check by next week after I get paid."

"This is getting old," Conrad said, sounding disgusted. "I agreed to let you keep the house after the divorce as long as you sent me monthly payments for my half. And lately, you haven't kept up your end of the bargain."

"I'm sorry. I'm doing my best."

"Yeah, but I have bills to pay too, you know. Just make sure you give me my check next week," Conrad said. "Or else I'm talking to my lawyer about taking you to court to change the agreement."

Mary angrily snapped the lid onto her tumbler. "Please don't. I want to keep this house."

"You should sell your mother's house and pay me back. She's never getting out of that nursing home, so why keep it?"

"If I sell her house, it will all go to the state for her long-term care," Mary said. "And she may still get better. She'll need a home to go back to."

Conrad laughed. "The way you tell it, she's practically a vegetable. She's not going home, believe me."

Mary bit her lip and remained silent. She knew Conrad was right, but she hated to admit it.

"Just get me my check, okay?" He hung up before she could respond.

Mary's heart pounded with anger, so she took several deep breaths and let them out slowly. Looking up at the glass in the kitchen cabinets, she saw her reflection staring back. Her shoulder-length brown hair already looked messy, and the lines in her forehead made her look ten years older than her true age of thirty-six. The stress Conrad and her mother were putting on her was aging her quickly. Not to mention how her boss treated her.

"Boss! Now, I am late!" She rushed to the kitchen door and nearly tripped over her gray Persian cat, Cassie.

"Oh, sweetie. I'm so sorry." Mary bent down to quickly pet

Cassie. "I'm late. I fed you earlier. Be good and I'll be home at dinnertime." The cat merely stared at her with golden eyes.

Mary hurried out the door, locking it behind her. Jumping into her older black Ford Escape, she backed down her driveway onto the quiet street.

Mary stopped for a moment and studied her house. She loved the cottage-style home she and Conrad had purchased together the first year of their marriage. It was in an older neighborhood in St. Louis Park, a nice suburb not far from Minneapolis. All the homes had been built in the 1940s but were kept up nicely. The stone chimney in front gave it a warm, cozy appearance, and the peaked roof was charming. Inside, it had original hardwood floors and beautiful woodwork. She didn't want to lose this house.

The fact that it was only a block away from her mother's house had sealed the deal when they'd purchased it. Who knew that one convenience for her would be the thing that would end her marriage?

Mary lived only one and a half miles from her work, but in the morning traffic, it took her fifteen to thirty minutes to get there. She pulled into the large parking lot behind the office and hurried to the back door. She'd driven faster than normal but made it to work on time.

Mary worked at Kerrigan, Clark, and Cunningham Accounting firm. The offices were set in a newer brick building that also held offices for a group of lawyers next door. Walking through the back door, she was greeted by blinding fluorescent lights that made her squint until her eyes adjusted. The office's main floor was filled with cubicles, and along the edges were tiny, windowless box-like offices for the people like her who worked directly under one of the main accountants. The owners each had large offices near the front, with extra-large windows for plenty of light.

Mary hurried down the hallway in her stout-heeled shoes to her tiny office, but just before she entered it, a deep male voice called her name from behind.

"Mary. Do you have the Halverson file ready? I have a meeting with him at nine-thirty." Mary turned to see Randall Kerrigan standing behind her. He was six feet tall, which meant she had to look up at him, and his eyes didn't stare at her, they bore into her. She'd been working under Mr. Kerrigan for twelve years, and he still seemed as stiff around her as the day she started there.

"Yes, Mr. Kerrigan. I have it on my desk. I'll get it for you." Mary rushed into her box of an office and picked up a folder with the name Halverson on it. "Here you are, sir," she said, handing it to him."

"Good. I'll also need Mr. Hernandez's reports by eleven. Make sure they're on my desk fifteen minutes prior to that." Mr. Kerrigan spun on the heel of his polished black shoes and left the office without waiting for a response.

Mary watched him leave, wondering why, after all these years, she was so afraid of him. Through the years, she'd seen him being friendly with employees, especially the women. But with her, he was always direct and short-tempered. She had no idea why.

But then, Mary was plain compared to the other women in the office who wore brightly colored dresses and suits with tall heels, had their hair styled nicely, and wore make-up. Mary had never been much for style, so her clothes were more functional and comfortable, but she was a good worker. Wasn't it more important to be a conscientious worker than a fashion plate?

Your personality is as drab as your clothes. Mary's mother's voice rattled inside her head. Her mother always had something negative to say about everything in Mary's life. It was hard to quiet her voice from her mind.

Mary sat in her office working on several accounts until ten forty-five, then hurried to Mr. Kerrigan's office with the Hernandez file. She glanced quickly into the office before entering, not wanting to disrupt a meeting.

"Here's the Hernandez file," she said cheerfully.

Mr. Kerrigan didn't even look up. "Good. Set it on my desk."

Mary stood there for a moment, unsure of what to do. She wanted to ask her boss a question, but he looked busy.

"Is there something you wanted?" Mr. Kerrigan asked, annoyed.

"I'm sorry to bother you, Mr. Kerrigan, but I wondered if we could talk for a moment." Mary's heart was racing.

"You've got three minutes," he said, glancing at the clock in the room.

Mary continued to stand. She'd read somewhere that you show more strength if you stand instead of sitting down. "Now that Gregg is leaving the firm, I wondered if you've thought about who'd fill his position." Gregg was a senior accountant in the firm while Mary was still only a staff accountant. She hoped since she now had her CPA it would give her an opportunity to move up.

Mr. Kerrigan frowned. "Are you thinking you'd like to have the senior accounting position?"

"Yes, sir," she said, trying to quell her excitement. "I've been with the firm for twelve years and earned my CPA. I'd love the chance to move up."

Mr. Kerrigan looked her up and down. Then he shook his head. "We're not filling that position once Gregg leaves. Or any others in the next couple of years. This economy is killing our business, and with everyone buying computer programs to do their finances and taxes, we've lost several clients. So, there won't be any advancement for a while." He returned to the paperwork on his desk.

Mary's heart sank. "Thank you, Mr. Kerrigan," she said quietly, walking slowly across the main floor toward her tiny office. She'd been hoping to finally have a chance to get a promotion and a raise after all these years, but it wasn't going to happen. And finding another job wasn't an option either. Not as long as she owed Conrad for his half of the house.

"Hi, Mary. How's it going today?" Janice Wilton smiled brightly at her.

"Oh, hi Janice," Mary said. "It's okay. How's your day?" Mary didn't like complaining about work to anyone. It didn't look good for an employee to complain.

"My day's going fine." Janice looked side to side and then said quietly, "Although Randall is in a bad mood today. I'd steer clear of him if I were you."

Mary would never call Mr. Kerrigan by his first name, but that was the difference between her and Janice. She was a pretty woman with long blond hair and big blue eyes. And she always wore stunning outfits—the style of clothes that Mary could never afford or dare to wear. But Janice was always friendly with Mary, and she appreciated it.

"You look nice today. I love your red suit," Mary told her.

"Oh, you're so sweet. Thank you," Janice said, smiling. "You know, we should go shopping together sometime. I know the best places to get clothes at a discounted price, and I'd love to help you update your wardrobe."

Mary looked down at the navy-blue suit she was wearing. Her clothes were usually monochromatic and oversized, because she preferred comfort over style. She'd never thought much about style and didn't have the money to buy new clothes. But sometimes, she did wish she dressed more like her co-workers. "Maybe we can do that someday," Mary said, not meaning a word of it. "I'd better go back to work."

"Okay. Have a great day." Janice gave her a little wave and walked down the hallway where Mary heard her greeting another employee.

Mary went to the breakroom at the back of the building and made herself a cup of coffee. Here, they had all the fancy coffee she couldn't afford at home, so she took advantage of it. It was going to be another long day of entering numbers into spreadsheets for clients that Mr. Kerrigan would take credit for, so she'd need all the coffee she could get to stay awake.

CHAPTER TWO

As five o'clock grew near, Mary neatly stacked the file folders on her desk and powered down her computer. She always tried to leave work at five with everyone else because she didn't like walking out to the parking lot in back alone. Of course, there were many nights when her boss asked, no, told, her at the last minute that he needed something ready by morning, and she stayed late. Hopefully, that wouldn't happen tonight.

Exactly at five, Mary turned out the lights in her office, shut the door, and filed down the hallway with the other employees. Once in her car, she drove the three miles in evening traffic to her mother's nursing home. Every night she went there to feed Abby dinner and visit, even though it was a one-sided conversation.

Mary's mother, Abigail James, was only fifty-nine years old, but because of poor lifestyle choices—smoking, drinking heavily, and eating poorly—she'd aged quicker than others her age. And then, after a tragic accident, she was left unable to care for herself.

Mary drove into the nursing home parking lot and found a spot near the door. She was thankful it was summer and would still be light out when she left. Mary hated walking around in the dark alone. It scared her.

The receptionist at the front counter waved at Mary as she walked past. Everyone here knew Mary because she was one of the few people who visited regularly. As she neared her mother's room, she took a deep breath. Before the accident, her mother had been difficult to get along with, but now, seeing her this way was even worse. Steeling herself, she entered the small room.

"Hi, sweetie." Judy Turner, Abby's older sister, stood there smiling. She had her purse in the crook of her arm and was near the door.

Mary adored her Aunt Judy. She was sweet and kind, the exact opposite of her mother. When Mary was younger, she'd secretly wished she could live with her Aunt Judy and her family, because they were all so nice. Mary and Judy even looked more like daughter and mother than she and her mother did.

"Hi, Aunt Judy. I'm surprised you're still here." Mary smiled back at her. Her aunt came every afternoon to feed Abby lunch and keep her company. The nurses were great, but they were also very busy and understaffed. Both Mary and Judy knew that Abby's meals would be rushed if they didn't help. "How is she today?"

"The same," Judy said. "And she didn't eat much of her lunch, so she may be extra hungry at dinner. She was less attentive than usual today."

Mary often wondered how Judy knew if her mother was attentive or not. Abby had broken her neck and spinal cord and had also hit her head badly when she'd fallen down the stairs.

She couldn't move or speak. The doctors said it was amazing that she could swallow food on her own. The only thing that did move were her dark brown eyes. And when they bore into you, it was scary.

"Thank you, Judy," Mary said softly. "I don't know what I'd do without your help."

Judy patted Mary's arm. "She's my sister, dear. I'm happy to help." She smiled again and left the room.

Mary set her purse on a chair and walked over to her mother. The room was private with one bed and a bathroom, but it was small. Aside from the bed near the room's one window, a television was attached to the wall and there were two chairs. Mary had tried to make the room cheery by hanging up pretty curtains and a few pictures on the walls from her mother's house. But it still looked sad.

"Hi, Mom," Mary said cheerfully. She noted that her dinner had already been delivered and sat on the tray by the bed. "I hope you're hungry. Your dinner sure smells good."

Abby rolled her eyes in Mary's direction, and her brows furrowed. Mary wasn't sure how much her mother understood. But sometimes, she was sure her mother understood everything. And if her mother could speak, she wouldn't have anything nice to say.

But then again, what else was new?

Mary went about the task of moving her mother's bed a little higher and then placing an absorbent bed pad over her mother from the chin down. She and the nurses had learned quickly that if Abby didn't like a certain food, she'd spit it out, and her blankets and nightgown were sprayed with food. A disposable bed pad worked perfectly to keep everything clean.

Mary moved the tray closer to the bed and took the covers

off the plates. All of her mother's food had to be pureed. Tonight looked like pureed carrots, chicken, and applesauce, all in separate little piles.

"It smells good," Mary said cheerfully. In truth, the smell in the room did not smell good at all. It had a sour smell mixed in with disinfectant.

Mary lifted a spoon of applesauce and placed it in her mother's mouth. She'd learned it was best to start with something sweet, then move on to the other foods. "Good, huh?" Mary asked.

Abby swallowed. The television was on with the sound down, and her mother's eyes were focused on the flashing images of an old 1970s sitcom.

It took half an hour, with Abby spitting out most of the pureed chicken, for Mary to finish feeding her. Honestly, if the staff could puree Doritos, chocolate cake, and mix in some Pepsi, her mother would eat it all.

A nurse came in exactly at six with a small cup of liquid medicine for Abby to drink. The older lady took it easily, because the staff knew to put a little sugar in it to make it taste better.

"That will help you sleep, Abby," the young nurse said cheerfully.

Mary frowned. Her mother had been in the nursing home for nearly eight months, and they always gave her sleeping medication. "Does she really need that medication?" she asked the nurse.

"We find that patients who lie around all day have trouble sleeping at night," the nurse said. "It's better for her if she can get a good night's sleep."

Mary nodded, and the nurse left. It seemed to her that it

was probably better for the night nurses to have everyone sleeping, not better for the patients. She immediately felt guilty for her thoughts. All the nurses had been kind to her mother, and it was the doctor who prescribed the medication. She shouldn't think badly of the staff.

When Abby was first brought to the nursing home after her terrible fall down the stairs, Mary had been told they would work with her to try to get her to move a little, even though her specialist had said she would never move again. But from what Mary could tell, all they did was move her around in the bed a few times a day to avoid bedsores and occasionally placed her in a wheelchair while they changed the sheets. No one, not even the doctor, believed Abby would ever move on her own again.

Mary slid the tray away from the bed and threw away the dirty pad her mother had sprayed food all over. Then she lowered her mother's bed a little. They usually left the television on until later in the night so Abby could watch until she fell asleep.

As Mary pulled the covers over Abby, she smiled down at her mother. "All tucked in," she said sweetly. "Just like Daddy used to say to me when I was little." She saw Abby's brows furrow and knew what she'd said made her angry. Her mother hated it when she and her older sister, Ginny, talked kindly about their father.

"It looks like I need to buy you a few new nightgowns," Mary said. "I'll do that this week. The washing machines here are brutal on your gowns."

Abby just stared at her.

"Have a good night, Mom," Mary said. "I hope you sleep well. I'll see you tomorrow evening." Mary never stayed long after her mother was given her medicine. She always dozed off quickly.

Walking out the door, she nearly ran into Amy Haskins, one of the regular night nurses.

"Hi, Mary," Amy said cheerfully. "Is your mama already sleeping?"

"Almost," Mary said. "She ate well tonight. Her food tray is still in there."

"We'll grab it when we check on her," Amy said.

Mary liked Amy. She was young with an upbeat personality and had a kind smile. Her short dark curls bounced as she walked, and her dark skin glowed with happiness. And Mary knew she was always kind to her mother.

"Well, I'll see you tomorrow night," Mary said.

"Just like clockwork," Amy said. "I swear, you're the only one who visits her mother regularly around here. I wish more family members were as attentive as you are."

"Thanks. I don't want my mom to feel alone. My Aunt Judy and I are all she has left who live around here," Mary told her.

"Are you an only child?" Amy asked.

"No. I have an older sister, but she moved to California years ago and has a family there, so she never comes home."

"Well, you're a good daughter." Amy patted her arm and then continued down the hallway.

Mary decided to make a quick stop at her mother's house on the way home to check on it and see if she had any other nightgowns. She drove the short distance to the St. Louis Park neighborhood, just a block from her house. Pulling into the driveway, she saw that the timer was working and the lamp in the living room had turned on. She always left the kitchen counter lights on, too. Their neighborhood was low on crime, but an empty-looking house could be tempting to a would-be robber.

Walking through the front door into the house, she locked the door behind her. Mary didn't like coming here or being alone in an empty house. Her house didn't bother her, but her mother's house—the house she'd been raised in—had an unwelcoming vibe.

Standing in the front entryway, she stopped at the foot of the stairs. This was where she'd found her mother lying on that fateful evening.

Mary had stopped by the house after work, as usual, to help her mother upstairs, change her into night clothes, and settle her into bed. Mary also made her a quick dinner before heading home. Her mother wasn't old by any means, but she'd mistreated her body for so long, she had trouble taking care of herself. Judy visited her in the afternoon and made her lunch, and Mary always got her settled in the evening. When she could no longer climb the stairs, Conrad had hooked up the stair-lift chair for her. But Abby never rode the chair when she was in the house alone because her balance wasn't good, and she could fall down the stairs at the top. Yet, for some reason, she'd taken the chair upstairs that evening, tripped, and fell, causing her injuries. Mary still didn't understand why Abby hadn't waited for her to come help her. And since her mother couldn't speak, she'd never know.

Taking a deep breath to calm herself, Mary climbed the stairs. At the top, she turned and slowly walked toward her mother's bedroom, turning on lights as she went. The first bedroom she passed was her old childhood room. She stopped for a moment and stared inside. Mary wished she could say she had happy memories in that room, but it would be a lie. Her mother was always yelling at her, calling her mean things like stupid, ugly, useless, lazy, and worthless. Even though Mary earned good grades in school and all her teachers liked her, Abby still put her down. Before her father died, he told her she was pretty and praised her good grades. He always smiled at her, teased her good-naturedly, and gave her plenty of hugs. But once he was gone, that all ended.

Passing her room, she walked by her older sister's room. Five years older than Mary, Ginny had always been the pretty one. With long blond hair and blue eyes, it didn't matter that her grades were average because she was not. All the boys in school adored her. But Ginny paid little attention to Mary, always pushing her aside or ignoring her. And even though Abby didn't ride Ginny as much as she did Mary, Ginny took off after high school graduation and never came home.

Finally, Mary flicked on the lights in her mother's room and stepped over the threshold. The room, like the entire house, was shabby. When her parents bought the house, it still had a seventies motif with gold shag carpeting and ugly finishes. Her father was handy—he worked as a carpenter for a living—but they never had enough money to remodel the older home. Some new paint here and there, fixes for leaky ceilings, or replacing the drafty window in the kitchen had been the most work done on the place. Mary had painted her bedroom pink as a teenager, and Ginny had painted hers red. But other than that, the home looked tired and worn.

She rushed in and pulled open one of Abby's dresser drawers. The wood screeched, echoing in the silent room. Chills ran up Mary's spine. She had never been allowed in her mother's bedroom as a child, and being there now made her anxiety rise. There were two older nightgowns in one drawer, and old underthings in the other drawer. Sighing, Mary left everything in its place. She'd have to stop at the mall on Saturday and buy her mother a few new gowns. Since Abby's disability money went directly to the nursing home to pay for her care, Mary paid for her mother's extra expenses. She didn't mind, but her money was tight, and buying extras made it worse.

Wanting to leave as quickly as possible, she hurried down the staircase. This house held too many sad memories, and she hated being here. She knew Conrad was right about selling it. But that would mean she'd have to go through everything and either pack it away or get rid of it, and that was a task she dreaded doing alone.

Mary stopped at the bottom of the stairs and glanced down the hallway to the back of the house. The dining room was there, with the scratched maple table and beat-up chairs. But there was something else in that room, and unable to stop herself, she walked in there and turned. There, a door stood, closed. It was the stairway leading to the unfinished basement, her father's favorite place to hide.

Mary had been twelve years old when her father fell down the basement stairs to his death.

Glenn James had been a hardworking, kind man who'd endured years of nagging from his wife. So, no one ever blamed him when he drank a little too much beer at night and sat in his basement workshop, building small projects no one ever used. As a young child, Mary understood that her father's basement refuge was just that—a place to escape from Abby. The girls were allowed down there any time they wanted. Mary sometimes went down to sit and watch her father cut small pieces of wood to piece together and make cutting boards or turntables for the kitchen table. He'd whistle along with the radio as it played old country music. Not the stuff they call country music today, but the legends like Johnny Cash, Hank Williams, and Waylon Jennings. But going downstairs to hang out with her father cost a price. When Mary came back upstairs, her mother would be meaner than normal.

Mary shivered as she thought about those days.

The evening her father died, Mary was upstairs in her bedroom, doing homework. Her sister Ginny said she was in the living room watching a sitcom, and her mother was in the kitchen. Ginny once told Mary that the night their father died, she'd run from the living room to the dining room and saw her mother standing at the top of the basement stairs, staring down at Glenn's immobile body.

"Well, call 911," Abby had said to her. "The drunken bastard finally killed himself."

That coarse statement from her mother made Mary wonder if her father had fallen or was pushed.

Mary shivered again and turned to leave. If ghosts existed, her father's spirit would be roaming the halls. And soon, so would her mother's.

As she reached the front door, her phone buzzed in her blazer pocket. She reached for it, thinking it was probably Conrad wanting to harass her for his money again. Instead, what she saw on the screen made her blood run cold.

"Creepy in there, isn't it?"

CHAPTER THREE

Mary had never felt so cold in her life. Even once she was safely locked inside her own home, she shivered. She ran to her bedroom and changed into sweats. It was summer and the temperature outside was seventy-seven, but she was chilled to the bone.

Heading back down the hall, she entered the kitchen and stared at her phone on the counter. Had she imagined the creepy message? And how did anyone know she was in her mother's house, standing by the very place where her father had died?

Slowly, she lifted her phone from the counter, and the screen came to life again. The message was still there.

"Creepy in there, isn't it?"

Mary swiped the message away, then thought better of it. She opened it up to see who had sent it. But there was no name, only a number she didn't recognize.

"It's just a coincidence," she told herself aloud. Yes, that was it. Just some random number texting scary things to people.

Suddenly, something grazed her ankle, and Mary jumped.

Looking down, she saw her cat, Cassie. "You scared me to death!" Mary lifted the chubby cat into her arms and hugged her. "I bet you're hungry. Come on. I'll feed you." Mary got a can of cat food out of the cupboard, opened it, and placed half inside Cassie's bowl. "There you go. Now I need to find something to eat."

Mary opened her fridge to see what was in there. Nothing, of course. She hadn't had a chance to pick up groceries in a while. Opening her freezer, she found two frozen diet meals. She picked the lasagna, pulled it out of the box, and placed it in the microwave. Once it was finished cooking, she sat down at her kitchen counter with a glass of iced tea and waited for it to cool.

Her nerves calmed as she sat in her kitchen. Unlike her mother's house, she and Conrad had updated this house. Conrad had a decent job as a mechanic at the local Ford dealership, and she'd made good money from her job over the years. When they married, they saved enough for a down payment and to improve their home. They remodeled the kitchen, sanded and stained all the hardwood floors in the house, and repainted each room. Her house was warm and cozy in beige and cream tones, and they'd chosen cushy furniture for the living room where they could nestle down on the sofa and watch television. They'd had such a great five years—or at least she'd thought it was great.

Sure, she had to stay late at work many nights, and she also had to go to her mother's house each evening to help her, but Mary thought Conrad was fine with that. But after a couple of years, the snide comments started about her not being home right away each evening and not being free on the weekends. Soon, the comments turned into fights between them. But what could she do? She had to care for her mother and she definitely couldn't tell her boss no if he asked her to stay late. Finally, Conrad told her to choose between him and her mother. Unfortunately, she couldn't choose, so he made the choice to leave.

The fact that he'd started sleeping with one of the car sales-people at work—an attractive redhead—had something to do with his leaving, too.

Mary ate her lasagna, then walked to the living room to watch television before bed. She made sure all the windows were locked, and the shades were drawn. The text message still gave her chills, and she couldn't stop thinking about it. Then she had a thought. Her sister Ginny may have sent the text as a joke. Mary quickly punched in her number from her favorites.

"Hello?" Ginny answered on the fourth ring.

"Hi, Ginny. Did you send me a text earlier?" Mary asked.

"Mary?"

"Yes," Mary said, sighing. Her sister knew it was her. Her name would have come up on Ginny's phone.

"Why would I have texted you?" Ginny asked.

"I don't know. I just got a creepy text earlier while I was at mom's house, and I thought you might have been playing a prank on me," Mary said.

"Eeww. You were at the old house? Why?" Ginny asked.

"I was getting some things for mom," Mary said. "But that's not the point. I wanted to make sure you weren't messing with me."

"Did it come from my number?" Ginny asked.

"Well, no. But I thought you might have done it from a

friend's number or used your husband's phone."

"Mary, do you really think with two kids, a job, and a husband, I have time to send prank texts to you?" Ginny asked, sounding annoyed.

Mary figured she didn't, but she'd hoped she had. She'd feel better if Ginny were messing with her instead of some random person sending them. "I guess not. How are the kids?"

"I'm actually at Trevor's soccer game right now," Ginny said.

"A soccer game this late?" Mary asked, looking at the clock. It was already after eight.

Ginny let out a long, drawn-out sigh. "It's two hours earlier here, remember?"

"Oh, yeah. Right." Mary felt stupid. Her sister had a way of making her feel that way.

"Listen, I have to go back to watch the game. I walked out into the parking lot to answer your call. I thought you were calling to say the old lady had finally expired."

Mary knew there was no love lost between Ginny and their mother, but she thought that was mean. "No. Mom is still hanging in there. I'll let you go."

"Okay." Ginny hesitated a moment. "But call me if you need anything, okay? I worry about you there all alone now that you and Conrad are divorced."

Mary was surprised. Ginny had always treated her as an annoyance. It was nice that she worried about her. "I will. Take care of those kids of yours, okay?"

"That's practically all I do. Bye."

"Bye."

Mary set the phone down and stared at the television. She wished she'd had the nerve to pack up and leave years ago like

Ginny had. Ginny had traveled to California all by herself, gotten a job, and then met her husband, Brent, while working as a waitress. Brent was doing his residency at the hospital across the street, and they started dating. Once he finished his residency, he was hired at a hospital in the ER, and they married. Then Trevor came along, and then Kayla. Mary had never met her sister's husband or kids and hoped someday she would. Maybe once her mother passed, she could take a trip to California.

Cassie joined Mary on the sofa and lay in her lap. As she stroked the cat's soft fur, Mary wished her life was different. She missed being married and having someone to spend her evenings with. She was thirty-six years old, unmarried, had no boyfriend, and had a job where there was no chance of a promotion. And she had a cat. Most people would think that was the bottom of the barrel.

She switched off the television. "Come on, Cassie. Time for bed," she told the cat as she stood. Turning off the lamp, she carried Cassie to her bedroom at the back of the house and went to bed.

* * *

The next morning, Mary was once again rushing to get out the door. She had her Yeti tumbler in one hand and her keys in the other when there was a knock on her front door. Mary sighed. Now what?

She ran to the front door and swung it open. A police officer stood there.

"Oh, Officer," Mary said, stunned. "What can I do for you?"

"Good morning, Ma'am," the young officer said. "Are you Mary Westin?"

"Yes. Yes, I am." She stared down at the tumbler in her hand. "Uh, I was just leaving for work."

"Sorry to hold you up, Mrs. Westin. My name is Officer Mark Bentley. Could I speak with you a moment?"

Mary studied him. He looked so young; like he was only in his twenties. Was he a real police officer, or someone pretending to be a police officer to get into her house?

"I'm sorry," Mary said. "But as I said, I'm just leaving. Can you talk to me out here?"

"Of course, Ma'am," the officer said. "I'm afraid I have bad news. Your husband was found deceased in his apartment this morning. I'm sorry."

Mary's mouth dropped open. Had she heard right? "Conrad is dead?"

"Yes, Ma'am," the officer said.

Why would anyone kill Conrad? He was just an average guy with an average job. And he lived in a decent neighborhood in a gated apartment building.

"How did it happen?" Mary asked.

"It might be best to talk about this inside," the officer said. He turned and waved to his partner in the patrol car behind him.

Mary hadn't even noticed the car and the other officer. She moved aside. "Yes. Please come inside."

The two officers passed her and walked into the living room. She closed the door and followed them inside. "Can you tell me what happened?" she asked.

Officer Bentley glanced around. "Do you live here alone?"

Mary set her tumbler on the coffee table and sat on the

sofa. "Yes. Well, except for my cat."

The officer nodded. They both remained standing. "Your husband," he started to say, but Mary interrupted him.

"Ex-husband. We're divorced."

"Oh, yes. Sorry. Well, your ex-husband was found on the floor of his apartment this morning by a Marissa Craig. She was picking him up for work," the officer said.

Conrad's girlfriend, the car salesperson, Mary thought.

"Miss Craig said she'd dropped him off at home last night and had gone home to her condo. Then this morning, he was found bludgeoned to death on his living room floor."

"Oh, my God!" Mary was shocked. "That's awful! Who would do such a thing?"

"We don't know yet, Mrs. Westin," Officer Bentley said. "That's why we're talking to everyone he knew."

Mary's eyes moved from one officer to the other. She couldn't believe anyone would kill Conrad so violently.

"When was the last time you saw your husband?" Officer Bentley asked as he pulled out a small notepad and pen from his pocket.

"My ex-husband," Mary repeated. "I haven't seen Conrad in over a month. He called me yesterday morning, but that's about all."

"What did he call you about?" the officer asked.

"I was late sending him my monthly payment for this house. But he was fine with me bringing it to him next week," Mary said quickly.

The officer frowned. "You owed him money?"

"It was in the divorce settlement," Mary said. "I wanted to keep the house, but I couldn't afford to buy him out, so he's taking monthly payments instead." After the words came out of her mouth, she realized that owing him money was a good reason to get rid of him.

"I see," Officer Bentley said. "And can you tell us where you were last night?"

Mary's heart beat wildly. His questions were making her nervous. "Well, I left work at five, then I drove to my mother's nursing home like I do every night. I was there until a little after six. I stopped at my mother's house for a few minutes after that. It's just a block away from here. Then I came home."

Officer Bentley stared directly at her. She noticed he had really blue eyes.

"And did you stay home for the rest of the evening?" he asked.

"Yes. I ate dinner and watched television. Then I called my sister who lives in California and talked for a while before going to bed."

Officer Bentley smiled at her and stood. "Thank you. If we learn anything else, we'll let you know."

Mary nearly jumped off the sofa, she was that relieved they were leaving. "Okay. And if you need any information about Conrad's family, let me know. Although I suppose Marissa has that information."

The other officer had already walked out the door, and Officer Bentley stopped and nodded. "Yes. She filled us in. By the way. Where do you work?"

"Oh. Only about a mile and a half from here. At Kerrigan, Clark, & Cunningham Accounting Firm."

"Okay. Thanks." He walked a short distance down her sidewalk, then turned. "Please don't leave town for a while. We might have more questions for you." With that, he turned and headed to his squad car.

Mary froze. Was she a suspect? On television, that's what they said to the main suspects.

Her phone buzzed in her pocket, and she lifted it out. There was a text c. She figured it was probably someone from her work wondering why she was late. Mary turned, walked back inside her house, and closed the door. Then she opened the text.

"Conrad deserved it. No more payments to him."

Chills ran through Mary's body as she read the text. Then she ran into the bathroom and threw up.

CHAPTER FOUR

Mary called her office to let them know she was running late. After that last creepy text, she wished she didn't have to go to work, but that would make Mr. Kerrigan angry. She had accounts to take care of for his clients.

As she drove the short distance to work, Mary thought of nothing but that awful text. It came from the same number as the first one, but she had no idea who was sending them. If someone thought it was a joke, they were dead wrong. The texts were putting Mary over the edge.

Mary had never wished Conrad dead. She was happy to pay him so she would own the house. But the more she thought about it, the more she realized how guilty that made her look. Yet, Conrad lived on the other side of town in a gated apartment building. There was no way she could have sneaked in and beaten him to death. Just the thought of it made her stomach lurch.

Mary parked in the back lot and hurried into the building. She was halfway to her office when Janice caught up with her.

"Mary! Oh, my goodness! Was that your husband who

was murdered last night?" Janice stood there in a bright yellow pantsuit with a floral blouse underneath. She looked so bright it hurt Mary's eyes.

"Ex-husband," Mary said. "Yes, it was." She frowned. "But how did you hear about it? Is it already on the news?"

"My boyfriend has a scanner so he can listen to what's happening in town," Janice said. "We heard about it this morning. I'm so sorry. It must have been a shock. He'd been beaten to death."

"It is awful," Mary said. "I really don't want to talk about it, okay?" She pushed past Janice and hurried to her office. Everyone was staring at her as she rushed by, and she just wanted to get away from their prying eyes.

Once inside her office, Mary took three deep breaths and let them out slowly. She didn't like being the center of attention. Janice must have told everyone in the office, and Mary hated the idea of people talking about her and Conrad's awful death.

Finally, she willed herself to calm down and sat at her desk. Turning on her computer, she pulled out the latest files from clients and prepared to enter their information.

"Mary!"

Mary jumped in her seat.

Mr. Kerrigan stood in her doorway; his eyebrows furrowed. "You were late this morning. I need the files from the Carlton and Dalton accounts, ASAP. I hope you've already updated them."

"Yes, sir," Mary said, her heart pumping wildly. He'd scared her, appearing suddenly in her doorway like that. "I have them right here. They're both updated." She stood and handed them to him.

"Good. And don't be late again. I don't know how you

expect a promotion when you're late for work," Mr. Kerrigan muttered.

"I'm sorry, sir," she said. "It couldn't be helped." But Mr. Kerrigan was already halfway down the hall by the time she'd finished her sentence.

Mary dropped back into her chair. Apparently, Janice's gossip hadn't reached Mr. Kerrigan's ears.

She worked all day and even ate lunch at her desk to make up for arriving late. It was hard to concentrate, though. All she could think about was Conrad lying dead in his living room. It was a horrible image she couldn't get out of her head.

She heaved a sigh of relief when five o'clock came and she could leave. She still had to go to the nursing home and feed her mother before she could go home. All she wanted to do was go home and relax in a warm bath to calm her nerves.

Then she remembered she'd promised to buy her mother some new nightgowns. Mary sighed. She should do that tonight so her mother would have them for the weekend.

Mary waited until the offices had emptied out before she left. She didn't want to talk to anyone about Conrad's death. She hurried to her car, got inside, and locked the door. Even though it was light out, it still scared her to be in the parking lot all by herself.

She drove to her mother's nursing home and hurried inside. The sooner she fed her mother, the sooner she could go to the mall to pick up nightgowns. Just as she left her car, her phone buzzed. Mary froze. Would it be another message from the stranger?

The buzzing continued. It was a call, not a text. She pulled her phone out of her pocket and saw it was her Aunt Judy calling.

"Oh, Mary," Aunt Judy said when she answered. "I just saw the news about Conrad. It's terrible. I'm so sorry."

Mary sighed. It was on the five o'clock news already. Now everyone would know.

"Thanks, Aunt Judy," Mary said. She was standing outside the door to the nursing home. "It was a shock. The police notified me this morning before I went to work."

"Oh, my. That's awful. Do they know who did it?"

"No, not yet," Mary said. "And since we're divorced, I'm not sure how much they'll keep me in the loop."

"Well, dear, you're in my thoughts," Judy said warmly. "Let me know if you'll need extra help with Abby. It's a lot for you to deal with right now."

"Thanks, Aunt Judy. I'm sure I'll still be coming here regularly, but thanks for the offer." They hung up, and Mary took a deep breath. She hoped the nurses hadn't heard the news yet.

Unfortunately, she was surrounded the moment she entered the facility.

"Oh, Mary!" the receptionist said, running up to her. Two other nurses came up to her, too. "We heard the news about your husband."

"Ex-husband," Mary said softly. It was getting annoying that everyone forgot they were divorced.

"Oh, of course," the receptionist said. "Have you heard anything? Who would have done such a thing?"

"I don't know anything yet," Mary said. She hated having all this attention. "But I'm sure the news will report it as soon as they know anything."

Everyone nodded and patted her on the back before heading back to work. Mary nearly ran down the hallway to get to her mother's room before being stopped again.

Once inside her mother's room, Mary closed the door. Abby's food tray was there, thank goodness, so she could hurry and feed her mother.

"Hi, Mom," Mary said, trying to calm her voice. "How are you feeling today?" Mary knew her mother couldn't speak, but Abby's eyes said it all. If she could talk, she'd make a snide remark like, *how do you think I'm feeling, trapped in this useless body?*

Mary placed a pad over her mother and then moved a chair closer to the bed. The television was on, and her mother's favorite show, *Wheel of Fortune,* was playing. Mary moved the food tray closer and lifted the lid.

"Looks good, Mom. Yams, peas, and chicken. And look," Mary lifted a sugar packet. "They remembered to give you sugar to mix into your yams, just the way you like them."

Mary mixed some sugar into Abby's yams and fed her small bites. Abby ate the yams, but when Mary tried to feed her the peas, she spit them out. Mary sighed.

"Mom, if you don't eat enough food, they'll have to insert a feeding tube, and you don't want that."

Abby narrowed her eyes at her.

Mary's phone buzzed, and she took it out of her pocket. Distractedly, she tapped on the text message, then sucked in a breath.

"Turn on the news. Now!"

It was another message from the creepy stranger. After reading it again, she picked up the TV remote and changed the channel to the local news.

"I saw the police at the apartment building across the

street, so I wondered if I had any video from my Ring camera," a middle-aged woman told the news reporter. "I was shocked at what I found around the same time as the murder." The video played, showing the front of a car parked within view and a woman getting out. The woman glanced around, even though the street was empty, then made her way across the street to the apartment building.

"Then, five minutes later, the camera caught this," the woman told the news reporter. The video showed the woman running across the street to the car, her head down, getting inside, then driving away.

"Have you given this to the police yet?" the reporter asked.

"No. But they can have it if they want it. All they have to do is ask," the woman said, looking like she was enjoying her five minutes of fame.

The reporter stepped in front of the news camera. "We've frozen the video of the unknown woman returning to her car so you can get a better look. If you think you know this woman, call the local police." They showed the frozen picture of the woman.

Mary's mouth fell open. The woman was too far away to see any facial features but she had dark hair and wore an oversized pantsuit. The car was black, but the license plate was unreadable.

The woman looked like Mary.

She quickly changed the channel back to the game show, but when she looked at her mother, she could tell her mother had understood what she'd seen on the news.

"Mom, I didn't kill Conrad. Someone else must have been angry at him," Mary said quickly.

Her mother's eyes grew even wider. She hadn't known that

Conrad was dead, of course, and they hadn't said it on the news.

"Someone killed Conrad last night, Mom. I'm sorry you had to hear it this way. But I was here with you and then went home, so it wasn't me," Mary insisted again.

Shaken up from the news report, Mary gave up feeding her mother. She quickly pushed the food tray away and lifted the pad off her mother. Abby's eyes bore into her the entire time.

The door opened and Amy walked inside. "Evening, Mary. I have Abby's medicine here," she said cheerfully.

"Good," Mary said, getting up and pushing her chair back. "I need to leave early tonight anyway."

Amy put the cup to Abby's lips, and she drank the small amount of liquid, but her eyes continued following Mary.

Mary moved away from the bed and picked up her purse. "Thanks, Amy. I'll see you tomorrow night." She was almost out the door when Amy called for her to wait.

Mary waited impatiently.

Amy walked up to her and said quietly, "I'm sorry about what happened to your ex-husband," she said. "It must have been a terrible shock."

Tears filled Mary's eyes. The compassion in Amy's voice had touched her. "Thank you. It was a shock."

"Well, dear," Amy said. "If you need anything, let me know. And I'll tell the other nurses that it's rude to gossip about it. I want you to feel comfortable coming here to help your mother."

"Thank you so much, Amy," Mary said, surprising herself when she reached out and hugged the other woman. "You can't imagine how hard this has been."

Amy patted her back and then gently pulled away. "I believe that. You take care of yourself, okay?"

Mary nodded and wiped her tears away with the back of her hand. "I will. Thank you."

Mary got inside her car and grabbed a tissue from the box she kept in there. This was all becoming too much. That video on the news had completely thrown her. Someone dressed like her and driving a black car like hers had been seen near Conrad's apartment the night of his death. Who could it have been? It certainly wasn't her.

And who was sending her the creepy messages? Mary thought momentarily about deleting the messages but then decided against it. Maybe, at some point, she'd need them to show the police that someone was stalking her. Instead, she looked at the information logo on the number's profile and blocked the person. There! They couldn't text her anymore.

Pulling herself together, Mary drove to the local mall and walked in through the closest entrance. The food court was there, and the smells drifting toward her suddenly reminded her she was hungry. Mary looked up and down the rows of vendors, then decided on a chicken strip basket from a little place that looked like a 1950s diner. Once her food was ready, she took it to a table far away from everyone else.

It was a Thursday night, so the mall wasn't too busy. Some teenagers were eating at the tables across the way from her, and a table of moms with strollers sat a few tables away. Mary thought they must be a group that meets regularly to have contact with other women.

Mary had wanted to have children when she and Conrad were together. First, they'd waited a couple of years so they could concentrate on fixing up their house. Then, when they did try, nothing happened. As time went on, Conrad became more irritated with her about the time she spent helping her mother. He'd even gone so far as to tell Mary she was being a doormat for her boss and her mother. They both bossed her around and took up her time, and she never complained. Mary hated being called a doormat, but deep down inside she believed Conrad was right. Mr. Kerrigan didn't appreciate the long nights Mary spent getting his work done. And her mother had never appreciated all the time Mary spent going to her house to help her or running errands. But by the time Mary realized Conrad was right, he had already left her.

Mary finished eating and walked the short distance to JCPenney to buy her mother's nightgowns. As she wandered through the lingerie department, she couldn't help but stop and admire the beautiful lacy nighties, teddies, and silky bras with matching panties. She'd never had the extra money to spend on luxury items like this. Practical clothing and underclothes made more sense to her. But maybe if she'd worn a sexy nightie occasionally, Conrad wouldn't have strayed. Or, maybe not.

She went to the aisle where they had the practical cotton nightgowns her mother preferred. Mary made sure they were long-sleeved, because even though the nursing home was warm, it seemed like her mother's body temperature was always cold. Mary picked out four in her mother's size, then walked past the pretty gowns again toward the check-out counter.

Stopping a moment in front of a short, red, see-through nightie with matching panties, she stared at it, trying to picture herself wearing such a thing. As she stood there, she realized there was a mirror on the pedestal behind the gown. Looking at her reflection, she felt deflated. She was plain, not pretty, and she had no sense of style. She wasn't like Janice at work, or any of the other women in her office. Sighing, Mary was about to turn away when she saw someone else in the mirror, far behind her. Mary frowned. The woman had brown hair just like hers and wore the exact same baggy brown pantsuit. And the woman was staring directly at her.

CHAPTER FIVE

Mary's heart thumped in her chest as she quickly turned, but there was no sign of the woman. She hurried to where she thought she'd seen the woman staring at her. But instead, she saw another post with a full-length mirror. Had she seen her reflection in the other mirror behind her? She walked closer and stared into the mirror, but she couldn't see her reflection in the mirror far behind her. Had it just been a weird coincidence?

Feeling unsettled, Mary hurried to the checkout counter and purchased the nightgowns. She practically ran through the food court to get outside to her car. Realizing it was now dark out, she hesitated in the entryway. She was so spooked from seeing someone who looked just like her that she didn't want to walk out to the dark parking lot alone.

Mary took a couple of deep breaths and let them out slowly. She could do this, she told herself. Then a group of young women walked through the entryway and out into the parking lot. Mary quickly went out with them. Luckily, their car was close to hers, so she didn't have to walk alone. Getting inside her little Ford, she quickly locked the doors and let out a long sigh of relief.

Once she arrived home, Mary turned on every light in the house, then thought better of it. It was easier for people to see inside with the lights on, even with the shades drawn. So, she turned down most of the lights, changed into comfortable clothes, and walked back into the kitchen.

A shadow darted in front of her, and she jumped. It took her a moment to realize it was her cat.

"You scared me, Cass," Mary said, lifting the fuzzy cat into her arms. "I'm late tonight, I know. I'm so sorry. Let's get your dinner."

Mary carried the cat to the refrigerator and pulled out a can of cat food. Then she set Cassie on the counter and spooned a pile of food into her bowl. Mary knew her mother would have a heart attack if she saw her feeding a cat on the kitchen counter. But Cassie's fur got everywhere anyway, so what did it matter? And Mary was always careful about wiping down the counter before cooking or eating.

With her kitty fed, Mary went into her living room and dropped on the sofa. She felt calmer now than she had at the mall. She rationalized that the person she saw in the mirror was her reflection. The mirrored posts must have been at the exact right angles so she could see herself in both. She highly doubted there was someone who looked just like her stalking her.

She glanced at her phone and was happy to see no new messages from the strange number. They had probably been prank calls. Now that she'd blocked the number, she was sure she wouldn't have any more problems with that caller.

As she scanned through shows on TV to find something to watch, Cassie came in and jumped on her lap. Mary petted the cat while clicking her remote. She was concentrating so hard on finding a show that she jumped when her phone rang. Cassie shot off her lap, scratching her leg.

"Damn!" Mary yelled. She looked down at her sweatpants; blood was slowly soaking through the fabric.

The phone kept ringing. Angrily, Mary grabbed it from the sofa and stared at the screen. The call was from the 612 area code. Who in the world did she know who lived in Minneapolis?

The phone stopped ringing, and Mary dropped it to her side. Her pants had a large blossom of blood on them now. She rolled up her pant leg and looked at the scratch. It was deep.

"Cassie! Are you trying to kill me?" she said to the cat. But Cassie had already run somewhere to hide.

Mary was just standing up to get a band-aid and antiseptic when her phone rang again. It was from the same number as before. She grabbed it and hit the red button. "Hello!"

"Hello. Is this Mary Westin?" an authoritative male voice asked.

"Yes," Mary said. Who on earth was calling her?

"Ms. Westin? My name is Detective Ryan Hodges with the Minneapolis Police Department. I've been assigned to the murder of Conrad Westin."

"Oh. Yes," Mary said, confused why they would assign someone from Minneapolis. "What can I do for you, Detective?"

"I'd like to speak with you tomorrow. Maybe in the morning?"

"I'm sorry, but I'll be at work tomorrow morning. I can't risk being late again," Mary said.

"Then what about lunchtime?"

"Well, I only get half an hour for lunch, but we can meet near my office," she said. The last thing she wanted was for a detective to show up at her work. The gossip would be terrible.

"Name the place and time, and I'll be there," Detective Hodges said.

Mary said she could meet him at twelve-thirty at the little coffee shop down the street from her building. Hopefully, it would be far enough away that her co-workers didn't go there.

"I'll see you tomorrow," the detective said, then hung up.

Mary went to her bathroom and found a bottle of rubbing alcohol and a band-aid. She rubbed a little of the alcohol on her scratch—which made her eyes water from the sting—then placed a band-aid over it. She'd learned from experience that cat scratches became infected if they weren't taken care of. Who knew what was on her cat's claws?

Mary tried to watch TV after that, but her mind kept wandering. She'd told the police everything she knew about Conrad's death, which was nothing. But then she remembered the video that was on the news. Would they really believe it was her? The woman's face was unrecognizable, and the license plates didn't show either. Besides, there were thousands of black cars in the area that looked like her Ford Escape. Maybe even hundreds of thousands. The police couldn't possibly think it was her.

Or could they?

Unable to enjoy the show she was watching, Mary turned it off and walked around, turning off the lights. She might as well go to bed. Unfortunately, sleep did not come easily.

* * *

Mary followed her normal routine the next morning and headed out to work. Today, she wore her nicest pantsuit. It had black pants with a white blazer that had black pinstripes. She wore a white blouse underneath. As she dressed, she wondered if her clothes would look better on her if she had them altered to fit her body. She imagined what her co-workers would think if she came in wearing clothes that weren't baggy.

"They'd probably think I'd lost my mind," she said aloud in her car, then chuckled.

Mary arrived at work and kept busy so she wouldn't think about her lunch meeting with the detective. Surprisingly, no one bothered her today, not even Janice. She hoped they hadn't seen the news story with the video of the mysterious woman near Conrad's apartment. If they had, they were probably afraid to go near her.

She hoped they hadn't. It was hard enough for her to make friends.

At twelve-twenty, she hurried out of the building through the front door and walked the short distance to the coffee shop. The place was busy when she arrived, but she found a small booth and ordered a Diet Coke while she waited.

Not long after, a tall, dark-haired man with a well-groomed beard and wearing a navy suit walked in and searched the place with bright blue eyes. Once he saw Mary, he made a beeline for her.

Mary was taken aback. She'd expected the detective to be older with a potbelly hanging over his belt buckle. But the man heading for her table looked in good shape and couldn't be much older than her.

"Mary Westin?" the man asked, looking down at her.

She nodded.

"I'm Detective Ryan Hodges." He nodded toward the booth. "Mind if I sit?"

"Oh, yes. Of course," Mary said, snapping herself out of her trance. Detective Hodges' face had a well-defined jawline underneath the beard, and his gorgeous blue eyes were fringed with dark lashes. "It's nice to meet you," she sputtered.

He smiled. "I know you have limited time, so I'll get right to it," he said. "I've been assigned to Conrad Westin's murder case. I know an officer already questioned you, but I just want to ask a few more questions."

"Okay," Mary said. She was so mesmerized by how handsome he was, it was hard to concentrate. She wished she'd put on a little make-up and worn something more fitted, even though she knew everything she owned was baggy. A man like Detective Hodges would be worth dressing up for.

He pulled out his phone and set it on the table. "I'm going to record our conversation. If you don't mind."

Mary looked at the phone for a moment. She'd better get her head on straight so she didn't say something stupid. "No, I don't mind."

"How long have you and Mr. Westin been divorced?" Detective Hodges asked.

"Almost a year. But he moved out about three months before he filed for divorce. He was living with his new girl-friend, Marissa."

"Marissa Craig?" he asked.

Mary nodded. "Yes."

The detective frowned. "But they weren't living together when he was killed, were they?"

Mary shrugged. "I don't know. He moved into the apart-ment a few months after he left me. I guess I didn't ask, because it didn't matter anymore."

"It must have hurt, him leaving you for another woman,"

the detective suggested.

"Of course. But I understood why he left. My job is demanding, and, well, my mother was too, and still is. He was tired of my being home late most nights."

The waitress came and asked Detective Hodges if he'd like anything. He ordered a black coffee.

"Aren't you going to eat?" he asked Mary. "My treat. It's your lunchtime after all."

"Well, maybe a blueberry muffin," Mary told the waitress. She left to get their order.

"Why was your mother so demanding?" the detective asked.

"Oh. My mom hasn't taken good care of herself through the years. So, she needed help getting up and down the stairs of her house, and I always helped her get settled in bed and made her dinner at night after work. My aunt helped her during the day."

"That was nice of you," Detective Hodges said. "Do you still help her?"

"She's in a nursing home now. My mom fell down the stairs a few months ago and is completely paralyzed. I go there after work each night to feed her dinner. So, yeah, I still do help her."

The waitress returned with her muffin and his coffee. Even though it was obvious that the waitress was much older than Hodges, she still smiled and flirted with him. Mary couldn't blame her.

"Have you ever been in Mr. Westin's apartment?" Detective Hodges asked.

Mary shook her head. "No. I've slid his check underneath his door a couple of times, but I've never been inside."

"Check?"

"Yes. I kept the house we owned together, so I have to pay him a monthly check for my half until it's paid off."

"Hm." Hodges took a sip of coffee. "So, now that he's gone, you won't owe him money anymore."

Mary had pulled apart her muffin and was about to place a piece in her mouth when he said that. She stopped her hand in mid-air. "I hadn't really thought about that. I'm not sure what will happen." She frowned. "I didn't kill Conrad so I wouldn't have to pay him off, if that's what you're thinking."

"Have you seen the video that was on the news last night? It was caught off a neighbor's Ring camera," Hodges said.

"Yes. I saw it. But that wasn't me," she said, growing angry. "You couldn't see a face, and a lot of people own black cars."

Hodges' brows rose. "You own a black car? What model?"

Mary took a breath. She had to stay calm or else she'd give more information than she meant to. "It's an older Ford Escape. Conrad found it for me at the dealership when we were married."

"I see," Hodges said. He took another sip of coffee.

Mary gave up trying to eat the muffin. Her nerves were frayed, and she wasn't hungry anyway.

Hodges leaned over the table, closer to her. "Mary," he said gently. "Is there any chance we'll find your fingerprints in Conrad's apartment?"

"No!" she said too quickly. "Like I said, I've never been in there."

"Not even on the hammer that killed him?"

Mary froze. Even though she'd known he'd been bludgeoned to death, she hadn't known the details. Conrad being killed with a hammer was too vivid a mental picture. Her stomach turned. "I didn't kill Conrad," she said softly. "I had no reason to. I was fine with paying him for his half of the house."

Hodges sat back in his seat. "Did you know that you're the sole beneficiary of Mr. Westin's life insurance policy he had at his workplace? You receive fifty-thousand dollars in the event of his death."

Mary's heart pounded. She knew she used to be the beneficiary of Conrad's life insurance policy, but she figured he would have changed that by now. "I had no idea," she said.

"The life insurance policy, the video, and the fact that you owed him a large amount of money points directly at you, Mary," Hodges said.

"No. I didn't kill Conrad. Look at me!" she said. "Do I look like someone who could pommel a man to death with a hammer?"

Detective Hodges stared at her for a moment, then switched off his phone recorder. "No, Mary. You look like a nice woman who works hard and cares for her invalid mother. You don't look like a murderer. Unfortunately, we have to follow the evidence."

Panic grew inside Mary. "Am I under arrest?"

Hodges smiled and shook his head. "No. But we need you to come down to the police station to be fingerprinted and to get a sample of your DNA. Would you agree to that?"

"Yes. Absolutely," Mary said. "Anything to clear myself so you can find Conrad's killer."

"Great." Hodges took one last sip of coffee, pulled his wallet out of his pocket, and dropped a twenty on the table. "I know you have to get back to work and then take care of your mother tonight. Can you come to the police station tomorrow?"

Mary nodded. "Yes. What time?" She just wanted to get this over with.

"Any time. Just tell them who you are and they'll know what needs to be done. Thank you for your time, Mary. I'll stay in touch." He stood, walked down the aisle, and went out the door.

Mary watched the detective leave, even as he walked outside and crossed the street. She turned to pick up her purse from the seat and caught sight of a woman outside staring at her through the window. The woman wore a baggy pantsuit just like hers, and her brown hair was messy from the wind. As Mary stared at her, she realized the woman's face looked just like hers.

Grabbing her purse, she rushed down the aisle, getting strange looks from the other customers. Out the door she flew, but when she turned left to where the woman had been standing, no one was there. She was gone.

Mary's phone buzzed.

She lifted her phone out of her pocket and stared at it. It showed a new text message. Mary swiped it open. In big letters it read:

"Don't block my number again, Mary. I'm watching you."

CHAPTER SIX

Mary was jumpy for the rest of the day. She tried to concentrate on work, but it was nearly impossible. Thank goodness it was Friday, and she'd have two days off.

Well, except tomorrow she had to be fingerprinted and have her DNA taken, as if that wasn't unnerving enough.

She thought about Detective Hodges. He was handsome, but he thought she was a killer. Her! Mary Westin! How could he ever think that?

And then there was that woman watching Mary. Mary knew the woman staring back at her through the diner's window was not a reflection or a figment of her imagination. She was a real person who looked and dressed like Mary. Someone was stalking her. But why?

As Mary entered numbers into spreadsheets, she wondered if the person stalking her was also the person who killed Conrad. Should she tell the detective about her stalker? And about the phone messages? Maybe that would prove that she wasn't the killer.

By five o'clock, Mary was ready to run out the door. She hurried down the hallway to the back door, praying Mr. Kerrigan wouldn't catch up to her to insist she return and work late. Once she was inside her car, she let out a sigh of relief.

A loud tap hit her car window, making her jump. Her heart beating fast, Mary turned toward the noise and saw it was only Janice standing there, smiling at her. Mary rolled down her window.

"Hi, Mary. I didn't mean to scare you. I just wondered if you wanted to grab a bite to eat and go shopping afterward. There's a great sale going on at Macy's."

Mary really wished she could go along with Janice. It would be fun to have a female friend to do things with. Unfortunately, she still had to stop by her mother's nursing home. "I wish I could," she told Janice. "It sounds like fun. But I have to take care of my mom at the nursing home and then head home. Maybe another time?"

"Oh, okay," Janice said, looking disappointed. "Isn't the nursing home supposed to take care of your mom? Isn't that what they're paid to do?"

"Yes," Mary said. "But they're so understaffed all the time. So, I make sure my mother eats dinner each night."

"Oh. That's so nice of you, Mary." Janice's smile returned. "Maybe we can hang out on a weekend sometime."

"I'd like that," Mary said. "Thanks for thinking about me."

"Sure. Enjoy your weekend." Janice walked away to her cute, sporty red car.

Mary watched her, feeling a little envious. She wished she were free to do as she pleased.

With another sigh, Mary drove away.

Once at the nursing home, Mary grabbed the bag of

nightgowns she'd purchased and headed inside. The receptionist waved as usual, and Mary walked down the long hallway
to her mother's room. When she opened the door, she was
surprised to see her Aunt Judy still there.

"Wow. You've been staying late a lot," Mary said. "Is everything okay?"

Judy smiled. "Abby was a little agitated today. I tried leaving earlier, but she was trying to shake her head. I don't know
what was happening. So, I told her I'd stay, and she calmed
down."

"Sorry," Mary said. "I hope Bruce doesn't mind you being
here so much."

"Oh, hon. My husband still works and couldn't care less
if I bring home something for dinner or make it. I'll just drop
by KFC or somewhere and grab dinner. Hopefully, Abby will
settle down tonight."

Mary set the bag down on the small dresser underneath the
television. "They give her sleeping medication at night, so that
will help."

Judy nodded. "What have you got there?"

Mary looked down at the bag. "I bought Mom a few new
nightgowns. Hers were starting to look a bit ragged. I washed
them before I brought them here."

Judy patted her gently on the arm. "You're a good daughter,
Mary. Abby is lucky to have you."

Mary looked into the kind face of her sweet aunt. If only
she knew just how mean her sister had been while Mary was
growing up. She'd be shocked that Mary showed up at all.

Judy left, and Mary placed her mother's nightgowns in one
of the drawers.

"I bought you some new night clothes, Mom," she said

aloud. "They're the ones you like." She walked over to the bed and saw the dinner tray there. "I hope you're hungry. Maybe you won't feel so anxious once you have something to eat."

The television was on Abby's favorite game show. Mary placed a pad over her mother's chest to protect her gown and blanket, then moved a chair closer. Lifting the lids off the food, she saw tonight was mashed potatoes, smashed carrots, and pureed brown stuff that she couldn't identify. Hamburger, maybe?

"Dinner looks good," Mary told her mother, even though it looked awful. "I'll put extra butter on your potatoes, just the way you like them." She turned and looked down at her mother's face and nearly jumped back. Her mother's head was turned toward her, and her dark eyes were wide and staring at her.

Mary took a breath. Obviously, the nurse forgot to straighten her mother's head after she repositioned her. Abby was unable to move her head and neck herself, so that was the only explanation.

Feeling creeped out at having to touch her mother, Mary gently moved her head so she was staring up at the television. "There, Mom. Now you can see the TV," Mary said, trying to sound calm, but she was shaking.

She fed her mother as much as Abby would allow, then cleaned her up. "I'll be here tomorrow afternoon, as usual," Mary said. As she moved the food tray away from the bed, someone knocked on the door twice, then came inside.

"Hi, Mary," Amy said cheerfully. "Time for your mom's meds."

"Hi, Amy," Mary said. "She just finished eating."

"Good." Amy walked around to the other side of the bed,

placed a hand under Mary's head, lifted it a bit, and then poured the liquid into her mouth. Abby swallowed.

"Are you doing anything fun this weekend?" Amy asked Mary.

Mary snorted. "Fun? I don't even know what that means anymore. No, I'll be here and then will probably clean my house and do laundry."

"I'm sorry, hon," Amy said sympathetically. "But what you're doing for your mom is so wonderful. Karma will pay you back, believe me."

Mary smiled. So far, karma hadn't been very nice to her. "I hope so."

Mary went home as usual, fed the cat, and changed into night clothes. It wasn't lost on her that her life was as boring and limited as her mother's life in the nursing home. Hopefully, someday, that would change.

* * *

The next morning, Mary was up, showered, and dressed early. She wanted to go to the police station and get it over with as soon as possible. Hopefully, giving them her fingerprints and DNA would eliminate her as a suspect, and she could stop worrying about being arrested.

The police station was a short drive from Mary's house. It was on a quiet street right next to City Hall. She pulled up to the brick structure and parked in front. As she walked up the short flight of steps, she suddenly felt nervous. She'd worn a pair of baggy jeans with a white cotton blouse and flats. When she opened the glass door, she quickly looked to see if a woman was standing behind her, watching her. Thankfully, no one was.

"Hi," she said to the person at the front desk. Her voice was tight with fear, and she had to clear her throat before continuing. "My name is Mary Westin. Detective Hodges asked me to come in."

The woman in uniform nodded and waved her down the hallway to the right. There, a young man in uniform met her and escorted her to a small room. He had her roll up her sleeves so she wouldn't get ink on her blouse, then rolled each inked finger on a sheet of paper with her typed information on it. Mary had thought getting fingerprinted would be strange, but the officer was so matter-of-fact about it that it was like a normal, everyday thing to do.

While she wiped the ink off her fingers, Detective Hodges walked into the room. "I'll take it from here," he told the officer, who nodded and left.

"Hi, Mary," Hodges said, smiling. "Do you mind if I call you Mary?"

Mary shrugged. "No. That's fine." She thought it was strange he was asking her permission now, considering he'd called her by her first name during their interview yesterday.

"I just need to swab the inside of your mouth for DNA," he said. He had her sit down in a chair while he slipped on sterile gloves. "Open wide." He moved closer to her and placed a long swab into her mouth that touched the inside of her cheek.

He was so close, Mary couldn't help but gaze into his blue eyes. Goodness, he was a good-looking man.

"Got it," the detective said. He placed the swab into a plastic container and snapped a lid on it. Then he placed a sticker on the case with her name on it.

"Is that everything?" Mary asked, standing. She rolled down her sleeves and buttoned the cuffs.

"Yes," Detective Hodges said. He smiled. "Would you like to go to lunch? My treat."

Mary was stunned. She hadn't expected an invitation to lunch from him. "Is this mandatory or just friendly?"

He chuckled. "Definitely not mandatory, although I would like to ask you a few more questions."

Mary considered it for a moment. She knew she was innocent, so what would it hurt to be treated to lunch by the handsome officer? "Sure."

"Great." He opened the door and led her outside to the back parking lot.

"Wait. My car is out front," she said, looking around.

"I figured I'd drive you, unless you'd rather take your car," Detective Hodges said.

"Oh, okay." Mary decided it wasn't a big deal. He could drop her back here after lunch. He opened the passenger door, and she slid inside.

He took her down the block to a chain restaurant, and they were led to a booth by the window. Once the waitress took their drink order and left, Detective Hodges spoke up.

"Do you mind if I ask you a few questions about your ex-husband?"

Mary pretended to look at the menu, even though she already knew what she wanted to order. She was just biding her time to gather her thoughts. Finally, she looked up and smiled at him. "Sure. That's fine."

"How long did you know him before you got married?" Hodges asked.

"About a year," Mary said. "I met him at the dealership when I took my mom's car in for an oil change. He told me that her brakes were bad and should be fixed. I told him my mother rarely drove anymore and would never pay for the repair, but I thanked him anyway. Then, we just started talking and he asked if I'd like to meet him for drinks some evening."

"So, it was love at first sight?" Hodges asked, smiling.

Mary chuckled. "No. But he was a nice guy, and a hard worker. He reminded me of my dad. He'd been a blue-collar worker, too. Just a nice, down-to-earth guy."

"Is your dad still alive?"

Mary's smile faded. "No. He died when I was twelve. He fell down our basement staircase."

"Oh, wow. That's terrible. I'm so sorry. That's strange, though, isn't it? I mean, didn't your mom fall down the staircase, too?" Hodges asked.

Mary hesitated. She hadn't realized the detective would know that. "Yes, she did. How did you know that?"

"From the EMT records, when the ambulance came to her house." Hodges looked her in the eyes. "I have to look at everything when I'm working a case."

"Of course," Mary said. Luckily, the waitress came and took their order. Mary ordered the salad with grilled chicken while Hodges ordered a cheeseburger with fries. After the waitress left, Mary spoke up. "Aren't you afraid of clogging your arteries with all that grease?"

Hodges laughed. "I guess I should be. But I have no wife to nag me or children to worry about, so I don't really think about it."

"You should still take care of yourself," Mary said, then felt embarrassed for saying it. It was none of her business.

Hodges turned serious again. "You're the one who found your mother at the foot of the stairs. Do you know how she fell?"

Mary sighed. "Not really. I went to her house each night after work to help her up the stairs and get her settled for the evening. Even though Conrad had installed a stair-lift chair for her, it was tricky at the top of the staircase. So, I'd wait for her upstairs and hold onto her when she left the chair so she wouldn't trip and fall. Except that night, she was impatient because I had to stay late at work. She must have tried going upstairs herself and fell after she stepped out at the top. The chair was at the top, so we know she went up."

"I see," Hodges said. "It's nice that you help your mother. I know a lot of people who wouldn't take the time to do that."

"It gets hard sometimes, though," Mary admitted. "I mean, helping my mother every night and on the weekends is what ruined my marriage."

"Conrad didn't like you being gone a lot?" Hodges asked.

Mary shrugged. "He knew when he married me that I had to help my mother, but I guess he got tired of it."

"I'm sorry," Hodges said. And when Mary looked up into his blue eyes, she could tell he meant it.

Their food came, and they both started eating. After a few bites, Hodges asked, "Do you know anyone who'd hate your ex-husband enough to beat him to death?"

Mary stopped chewing. The thought of Conrad's violent death made her stomach roll. "No. Most of his friends were from work, and they all got along well. You might want to ask his girlfriend, though. I haven't been close with Conrad for a long time."

After that, Hodges made normal conversation, asking Mary about her job and why she liked working in accounting.

"Numbers are exact," she said. "They have to add up, or you've made a mistake. There's no leeway in accounting. It's either right or wrong."

"And you like that?" he asked.

"I like the certainty of it. There's no guessing. It's not like people who you always have to try to figure out how they're feeling. It's just straight out facts," Mary said.

"Very matter-of-fact, like you," Hodges said.

Mary stopped eating and looked at him. "Yes. I'm not very good with nuances. I need people to tell me how they feel or what they want so I don't have to guess." She sighed. "That's why I don't have many friends. Women can be so tiresome with all their *feelings*. I just want people to tell me how they're feeling."

Hodges chuckled. "That's how my work is. We work on facts, not guessing. I sometimes wish people would say what they mean instead of constantly dancing around everything."

Mary set her fork down and stared straight at Hodges. "That's exactly what I've been telling you all along. The facts. I would never have hurt Conrad. I didn't have any reason to. That's the honest truth."

Hodges moved forward in his seat. "I believe you, Mary. And that's why I need your help finding his killer."

CHAPTER SEVEN

It was a relief to Mary that Detective Hodges believed her. But she had no idea how she could help him find Conrad's killer. All she could do was tell the truth.

After Hodges dropped her off at her car, Mary drove to her mother's nursing home. It was late afternoon, so she was surprised to see her Aunt Judy still in her mother's room when she arrived.

"Hi, Mary," Judy said cheerfully.

Mary was always amazed at how kind and giving her aunt was compared to her mother. Abby had been selfish and mean. How on earth could both women have grown up in the same family?

"Hi, Aunt Judy."

"I helped the nurse bathe and change Abby's nightdress this afternoon," Judy said. "She's wearing one of her new gowns."

"That's wonderful," Mary said, sounding more enthused than she felt. She had helped her mother clean up and change clothes many times while she still lived in her own home, and

Mary had hated it. But it had to be done. She was happy that was one thing she didn't have to do here.

Judy's expression turned serious. "Have they made any headway in finding Conrad's killer?" she asked quietly.

Mary shook her head. "No. In fact, I was just at lunch with the detective in charge of the case. He wanted a little more information about Conrad."

"It's terrible," Judy said, shaking her head. "A person isn't safe even in their own home."

Mary nodded. She felt that way when she was home alone, especially since she'd been seeing a woman following her around and someone sending her creepy texts.

"It is terrible. And some weird stuff has been happening to me lately," Mary confided in Judy. "I've been getting texts from someone I don't know, and I've also seen a woman who resembles me following me around." She shivered involuntarily. "I don't know what to make of it."

Judy's eyes grew wide. "Really? Did you share that with the detective?"

"No. I didn't think it had any relevance to Conrad's case."

Judy glanced over at her sister lying in bed, then back at Mary. She moved further away from the bed and motioned for Mary to come closer. "That is strange. Does the woman look your age, too?"

"She does. The first time I saw her was in a mirror, so I thought I had just seen my reflection. But the other time, it was out of the window. She was standing there, staring at me."

Judy frowned. "Don't you think it's a weird coincidence? I mean, considering your history."

"What do you mean?" Mary asked. She had no idea what her aunt was talking about.

"I mean, considering you were born with a twin," Judy said. "It seems kind of creepy that you're suddenly seeing someone who looks exactly like you."

Mary was so stunned, she wasn't sure she'd heard right. "Twin? I have a twin?"

"Oh, sweetie. Didn't you know?" Judy looked surprised. "I thought your parents would have told you when you got older. You were born with an identical twin. She died two days after your birth."

"What?"

"Well, dear. Who did you think was buried beside your father?"

Mary tried to think of the grave beside her father's, but nothing came to mind. If she'd even noticed it, she wouldn't have paid any attention. She'd been too upset about losing her father.

"I can't believe your mother didn't tell you. I suppose Ginny wasn't told either." Judy shook her head in disgust. "Your mother gave birth to twin girls, and you both were perfectly healthy. But then, for some strange reason, your twin died two days later. I visited Abby and saw both babies on the first day. You were both adorable. I could never understand why a healthy baby would die so suddenly."

"And the grave is next to my dad's?" Mary asked, still having trouble believing she had a twin.

"Yes. Such a sad thing, to have to bury a baby," Judy said. "But you know, the weird thing was your mom didn't even give the child her own name. The plaque only says Baby Mary. Now that's creepy. But then, your mother has always been a bit different."

"The dead baby has my name?" Mary asked, her voice

rising. "Why?"

Judy patted her arm. "Like I said, dear. Your mother has odd ideas." Judy was silent for a moment, but looked as if she wanted to say more.

"What is it?" Mary asked. "What else do you know?"

"Well, it was just something unnerving your mother said after the baby died. I went to visit her at the hospital, thinking she'd be devastated. But she just looked me in the eye and said, 'We could only afford one anyway.' I mean, who says something like that? I just marked it down to her being depressed after giving birth and losing a child."

Mary was still reeling from all the new information. But her mother's words didn't surprise her. That was exactly something her mother would say.

"I'm so sorry I had to be the one to tell you," Judy said. "But it's good that you know. It doesn't explain why someone is following you, though. It just seemed like an eerie coincidence."

Mary nodded. She glanced at her watch. It was two-thirty. She still had a couple of hours before her mother ate dinner.

"I'll walk you out, Aunt Judy," Mary offered. "I have an errand to run before I come back and help Mom with dinner."

"Okay."

She walked her Aunt Judy to her car and hugged her goodbye. "Thanks for telling me about my twin. I never would have known otherwise."

Judy nodded, got into her car, and drove away. Mary did the same. But she wasn't headed home; she was heading to the cemetery.

It took Mary twenty minutes to reach the cemetery where her father was buried. She didn't visit his grave often and felt guilty about it. Her mother had drilled into her that dead people weren't waiting in cemeteries for a visit, and Mary sort of agreed with that. She thought about her dad often, which was better than visiting a plot of land.

Mary drove around the cemetery until she found the area where her father was. She pulled to the side of the road and parked, then got out of the car and walked toward the grave. Even though she'd only visited a few times, she knew exactly where he was buried. It had been ingrained in her twelve-year-old brain because his death and funeral were the most tragic times of her life.

As she drew closer to his grave, she was surprised to see fresh flowers there. Who had visited her father's grave? Maybe an old friend or co-worker. Then she thought of Aunt Judy and decided it must have been her. The closer she got, the more nervous she became. She wasn't nervous about her father's grave, but because of the grave next to his. And to her surprise, there were flowers on that grave, too.

Mary's heart pounded as she neared the grave on the left of her father's. The marker was a flat one that set into the ground, and it looked old. On it read: Baby Mary—Born: March 10, 1989, Died: March 12, 1989. There was no last name.

She stared at her twin sister's grave and wondered what it would have been like to have grown up with a sister her own age. Someone who not only looked like her, but maybe even thought like her. Someone she could have been close to. Maybe even best friends with. Tears filled her eyes at the loss of her twin, but also the loss of a companion Mary could have had her entire life.

It was eerie, though, that her parents had named the deceased twin Mary. Had her mother been that lazy not to think of another name for her baby?

Chills ran up her spine as she stared at the grave. She walked over to her father's plot and looked at his plaque. He'd only been thirty-five years old when he died. Mary was one year older than that right now. At thirty-five, her father had already given up on being happy and lost himself in bottles of beer. Her mother had broken him, and Mary knew he only stayed with her to support his girls. It made her sad that her father had such a terrible life.

"I'm sorry, Dad," she said softly. "She should have been nicer to you. To all of us. I miss you."

Backing away, Mary glanced again at her twin's grave. She hoped her father and twin sister were together. Mary wasn't sure if she believed in an afterlife, but she hoped that if there were one, they'd find each other. She turned and walked quickly to her car. This was just too much sadness for one day.

Mary drove back to the nursing home and fed her mother dinner. The whole time, she pretended to be cheerful even though she wanted to scream at her mother for all the pain she'd caused everyone. But honestly, yelling at her wouldn't change things. Nothing Mary did now could change things. So, she fed her mother, cleaned her up, and then left after the weekend night nurse gave Abby her sleeping medicine.

As she drove home, a thought came to her. Maybe her mother had kept her twin's birth and death certificates. She could stop by her mother's house and see if she could find them.

Mary pulled up to the house, glad to see the timer was still working and the lights were on inside. It wasn't dark yet, but Mary still hated walking into a dark, empty house. The lights made her feel safer.

She got her key, opened the door, then quickly walked inside and locked the door behind her. She didn't know where her fear of entering an empty house came from. Maybe because her sister Ginny used to scare her sometimes when the lights were out at night. Or maybe because her father had fallen down a darkened set of stairs. Whatever caused it, her heart always beat faster when she entered this house alone.

Mary stood in the entryway, wondering where her mother kept her important papers. Maybe on the top shelf of her closet? She hoped it wasn't stored in a box in the basement. There was no way she was going down there.

She headed upstairs and hurried down the hallway toward her mother's room. As she passed Ginny's old bedroom, she paused. The room was dark, but she noticed the bedspread looked messy. She reached in and flicked on the light. The bedspread looked like someone had been sitting on it. But that was impossible. Mary was the only person who had a key to this house.

"Maybe I only thought the bedspread looked smooth the last time I saw it," she said aloud. Her voice echoed in the empty house. Snapping off the light, she moved quickly to her mother's bedroom.

Looking around, she opened the nightstand drawer by her mother's bed to see if the papers were there. She saw nothing besides cough drops and reading glasses, so she turned and walked to the closet. Opening the folding doors, she looked up at the shelves. Her mother was in no way a hoarder of clothes or shoes, so her closet wasn't very full. The shelves, however, held old paperback books, shoe boxes marked with different years of tax receipts, and a basket of scarves and gloves. To the far left, she saw a very old shoebox, but nothing was written on it. Mary reached up and pulled the box down, taking it to the bed.

Sitting gingerly on the bed, Mary opened the lid. Inside, she saw folded pieces of paper that looked like legal-size documents. Mary took a deep breath. She lifted out one envelope and pulled out the sheet of paper. It was her father's death certificate. She hoped that if that was in this box, her sister's papers would be in there also.

She sifted through a few more envelopes. She saw the deed to the house, house insurance forms, and an envelope of old school pictures of her and Ginny. Her sister was five years older than her, so Mary had never seen photos of Ginny in the first and second grades. Abby hadn't been one to scrapbook, so pics were usually tossed in shoe boxes and stashed away.

Mary studied the photo of her sister in the first grade. Even though her sister had blond hair, Mary was surprised that Ginny looked much like she did when she was younger. The same eyes—except Ginny's were blue—the same nose and mouth. But as they grew older, they couldn't have looked more different than if they'd been from two different families.

Setting aside the photos, Mary reached for another envelope. This one looked older. She carefully pulled out the first sheet of paper the envelope held. Opening it, Mary gasped. It was her twin's birth certificate. Mary Jane James, born March 10, 1989. The hospital's name and address, as well as the doctor's name, were on the certificate.

Mary did have a twin sister. But why on earth had they named her Mary too? She knew it wasn't her birth certificate because she had hers at home, and her middle name was Elizabeth.

Pulling out the other sheet of paper, Mary saw it was her sister's death certificate. Mary Jane James, died March 12, 1989.

It was all so surreal.

Mary slipped the papers into the envelope and returned them to the box. She decided to take the box home with her. These were important papers that needed to be kept somewhere safe, not in an empty house where anything could happen.

She hurried downstairs and was about to open the front door when she heard a thump at the back of the house. Mary froze. Someone was in the house. She stood and listened, hoping it had been her imagination. Another thump came from the dining room. Terrified, Mary ran out the front door and to her car. She locked herself inside, quickly pulled out her phone, and called Detective Hodges.

"Mary? Is everything okay?" Hodges asked. At his request, they'd traded phone numbers in case she remembered something or needed his help.

"There's someone in my mother's house," she said hoarsely. She was so terrified; she could hardly speak.

"Are you in the house right now?" he asked.

Mary could tell he was moving around, possibly already running to his car. "I was in the house but ran out to my car and locked the door. Should I call 911?"

"No. I'll be there shortly. Give me the address."

Mary told him the address, and he said he'd be there in five minutes. She thought he lived in Minneapolis, but apparently, he was staying somewhere nearby.

As promised, Detective Hodges arrived quickly. She rolled down her window as he came up beside the car.

"Where did you hear the noise?" he asked.

"At the back of the house, near the dining room and kitchen. It was two loud thumps."

"Okay. Is the front door locked?"

She shook her head. "No. I was so scared, I just ran out of the door."

"I'll go check it out," Hodges said, pulling his gun from inside his jacket. "Don't come in until I give you the all-clear."

Mary nodded again. There was no way she was going inside that house. She hoped Detective Hodges would be safe and wished he'd called for backup.

For ten long minutes, she watched from her car as lights were turned on inside the house. Then, slowly, the lights were turned off, and soon the detective came out of the front door. He walked to the car and got in the passenger seat.

"This car is small," he said, glancing around. There was barely enough headroom for him.

Mary stared at him. "What happened in there?"

"Oh." He chuckled. "Nothing happened. I didn't find anyone inside the house. But I did find the kitchen door unlocked, and the screen door unhooked. It banged in the wind several times while I was in the house. So, I snapped the screen door closed, locked it, and then locked the back door, too."

"Unlocked? I never leave anything unlocked. I'm a stickler for locking windows and doors."

"Maybe you forgot to lock it," Hodges said. "Or, maybe you thought you did, and it didn't catch. The only other reason would be if someone else has a key."

Mary shook her head. "No one has a key except for me and my Aunt Judy, and her key is for the front door. But she has no reason to go inside the house now that my mom doesn't live there anymore."

"You might want to ask her anyway, just in case," Hodges said. "Another reason would be if a squatter is living inside your mother's house. But I didn't see any sign of a broken window for access or that anyone was living in there."

A squatter. Mary hadn't thought about that, but she knew it happened when people left homes empty. As she considered that, she caught a whiff of Hodge's aftershave. It smelled spicy, which suited him. Even though he always wore a suit, he looked like the kind of guy who enjoyed the outdoors and would go camping and fishing. She had never been the outdoorsy type, but she would try it if she had someone like him to go with.

"The next time you need to check on your mother's place, why don't you call me first?" Hodges said, catching Mary's attention. "I don't want you going in there alone."

"Oh, okay." Mary pushed thoughts of camping with Hodges from her mind. "Thanks. And thanks so much for coming here tonight. I was really scared."

He smiled. "You're welcome. Do you want me to follow you home to make sure you get inside okay?"

"I just live down the block," she said. "And I can pull right up to the kitchen door in the driveway. I'll be fine."

"Okay. Have a good night." He stepped out of her car and closed the door.

Mary started the car and pulled slowly out of her parking spot. Even when she was down at the stop sign on the corner, she saw Hodges still standing on the curb. She wasn't sure if that made her feel safe or creeped her out that he was watching her.

CHAPTER EIGHT

As soon as Mary stepped inside her house, she locked the side door and ran to the front door to make sure it was locked. She walked to the living room to pull the shades and saw a full-sized SUV drive slowly down her street. It took a moment to realize it was Detective Hodges' car. He was making sure she got inside safely.

She pulled the second shade and turned, nearly tripping on Cassie.

"Sheesh!" Mary said, bending to pick up the cat. "You're too sneaky."

Cassie purred happily in her arms.

Mary entered the kitchen and poured canned cat food into Cassie's dish. "There. You're fed. Now I just need something to eat."

First, she went to her bedroom, pulled those shades, and then changed into comfy sweats. Returning to the kitchen, Mary stared at the contents of her fridge. She still hadn't had a chance to go to the grocery store, and it was slim pickings. She decided to heat up a frozen shrimp pasta diet meal from the freezer and hoped it wasn't too old. Then she sat at the counter next to her cat.

"We may need to get a dog. A really big one," she told Cassie. "It's just too scary living alone." When her food was ready, she sat again at the counter to eat it. As she ate, she decided to call her sister and ask her if she knew about her twin.

Ginny answered the call after five rings. "Hey, Mary. Calling me is getting to be a habit."

"Sorry," Mary said. "I know you're busy with the kids, but I learned something interesting today."

"What was that?" Ginny asked.

"Your voice sounds muffled, like you're in a closet," Mary said.

"I practically am in a closet. I went into the changing room at Kayla's ballet class so I wouldn't bother the other moms with my call."

"Oh. Sorry. I just wanted to ask if you knew I was born with a twin sister?"

"What?" Ginny sounded shocked.

"It's true. Aunt Judy told me about her today. Isn't it freaky that mom or dad never told us? Her grave is right next to Dad's, and I didn't even know it," Mary said.

"Did the baby die at birth?" Ginny asked.

"No. Judy said it was really strange. She saw me and my twin the day we were born, and she said we both looked healthy. But the next day, while mom was holding the twin, the baby died." Mary got chills just talking about it. "Judy thought that was odd."

"That is weird," Ginny said. "But then again, I was only

five when you were born, so they wouldn't have told me a baby died. I guess they never thought it was worth bringing up."

"I suppose not," Mary said. "Still, our lives would have been so different if I had a twin."

Ginny laughed. "Yeah. I would have had two of you to put up with. But Mom would still have been the mean old lady that she is. That wouldn't have changed."

"That's true."

"Say, class is almost over, so I have to go. If you learn anything else about our deranged family, let me know, okay?"

"Okay. I'm not sure there's much else to know, though. Talk to you later." Mary hung up. She wished she could visit Ginny and her family. She hadn't seen her sister since she left home at age seventeen. It was lonely not having any family around.

As Mary got ready for bed, she thought about her twin and wondered why the baby died. She also thought about Aunt Judy's comment that her mother said they could only afford one baby. That sounded like something cold her mother would say, but still, how could she not have been bereaved over losing one of her babies?

Mary also noticed there was no cause of death listed on the baby's death certificate. Wasn't that mandatory?

Tomorrow, she was going to research the hospital where she was born and the doctor who delivered her and her sister. She wanted to learn more about what happened.

As Mary lay in bed with Cassie beside her, purring, she couldn't help but think about Detective Hodges. He was very handsome, and he smelled good tonight. She liked that he came to help her when she was frightened at the house. He didn't have to do that. He could have sent a patrol car over. But he did, and he didn't seem bothered by it.

She had to admit, she liked him.

But why would he even look twice at her?

Conrad had always looked past the fact that she wasn't a beauty queen, didn't wear a lot of make-up, or dress sexy. Mary had always considered herself to be plain, and she'd accepted that a long time ago. But maybe if she put a little more effort into how she looked, someone like Detective Hodges would look at her differently.

Or was that all just silly?

But it would be so nice to have a man in her life again.

* * *

The next morning, Mary opened her computer and searched for the hospital in St. Paul where she was born. Her parents had lived in a small apartment back then and hadn't had much money. The hospital was no longer listed, but after more research, she found it had been taken over by one of the big hospitals. The doctor had also practiced at the newer hospital but had long since retired.

Mary decided she'd take a long lunch break on Monday and go to the hospital to see if she could learn any new information about her deceased sister. It was a long shot, but she had to try.

She'd just closed her laptop when a message buzzed on her phone. It was from Detective Hodges.

Conrad Westin's funeral services will be on Tuesday at three p.m. I thought you'd want to know.

Mary definitely wanted to attend Conrad's funeral. After all, she'd been married to him for five years. It would be odd if she didn't attend. But as she thought about the service, she wondered what she'd wear. She had several dark suits, but they were all baggy. She really wanted to get some clothes that fit her better. It was time to stop looking dumpy and start living again.

"I'm going shopping," she told Cassie.

She drove to the mall and parked close to her favorite department store. Walking inside, she wandered around the women's clothing section, looking for business attire. Finally, she found the area that sold women's suits and dresses.

Mary looked through the suits for something to wear to the funeral. She saw a fitted black jacket next to a pair of pinstripe dress pants. Beside it was a pinstripe skirt. She pulled that off the rack and held it up against her. It was just above the knee, shorter than her usual skirts.

"That would look lovely with this blouse," a saleswoman said, lifting a white blouse with large black flowers printed on it off another rack.

Mary considered the blouse. It looked soft and billowy. "I like it," she told the woman. "I want to try this entire suit on, but can you give me more suggestions for tops to wear underneath?"

The saleswoman was happy to. Soon, Mary had a dressing room full of blouses, short-sleeved sweaters, jackets, pants, and skirts to try on.

"And here's a pair of black pumps you can use to try the clothes with," the woman said, handing her a pair of leather shoes from the shoe department. "That way, you can tell what length you need the pants to be."

Mary tried on everything. She'd been wearing baggy suits for so long, she was surprised she still had a nice figure under all her clothes. The fitted jackets looked great, and she tried on a red sweater underneath. She'd always looked good in red but never bought it. It didn't seem like a color for work. But Janice and the other women at her work always wore bright colors, so why shouldn't she?

In the end, Mary bought two new suits, each with matching slacks and skirts, and four new tops. She even bought the leather pumps because all her shoes were short-heeled and boxy.

She felt like a new woman.

The minute she left the store and placed her purchases in the car, she felt guilty. There was no way she would have been able to buy these clothes if she were still paying Conrad for his half of the house. Did enjoying having the extra money make her a bad person?

On the way to the grocery store, Mary told herself she deserved new clothes. She hadn't bought anything for herself in years, and even Conrad had commented that her wardrobe was starting to look dumpy the last year they were married. She wasn't hurting anyone by trying to look nice again.

Mary filled her grocery cart with fresh fruit and vegetables and bought a few frozen diet meals for when she didn't want to cook. She wanted to eat more salads and fruit to feel healthier. She hadn't been putting herself first for a long time, and she decided it was high time she did. After all, she wasn't getting any younger, and she needed to take care of herself.

That evening, Mary arrived at the nursing home in good spirits. Mary felt better about herself than she had in years. She was turning over a new leaf and going to join in on life instead of hiding from it like she had since her divorce. She entered her mother's room five minutes after five and was surprised that her dinner hadn't arrived yet.

"Hi, Mom," Mary said cheerfully. She'd even put on a little mascara and lipstick tonight. "I see they haven't brought your food yet. So, I guess we can watch TV while we wait."

When Mary looked down at her mother, she was taken aback. Her mother's eyes were wide, almost fearful. Abby did a good job of expressing herself with her dark eyes.

"What's wrong? Did something happen today?" Mary asked her mother. Of course, all her mother could do was stare back at her.

Mary's heart quickened. Her mother looked scared to death.

"Let's put on a nice comedy show for you," Mary said. There were no reruns of *Wheel of Fortune* on Sunday nights, so Mary searched the channels for an old sitcom. She found *Friends* and left it on there, even though it hadn't been a show her mother ever watched.

"I'll go check on your dinner, okay?" Mary said. She went out the door in search of the evening nurse.

"Oh, hi, Mary. Did you forget something?" Kari, the weekend night nurse, asked when Mary walked up to her.

Mary frowned. "Forget something? No. I was wondering when my mom's dinner would be ready."

Kari was a pretty young woman who was always full of smiles. But right now, she stared at Mary as if she'd lost her mind. "Dinner? You already fed your mother her dinner. You asked me for it earlier because you said you had to be somewhere tonight."

Mary was confused. "So, someone already fed my mother dinner?"

Kari's expression turned wary. "Not someone. You. You fed your mother her dinner half an hour ago. I saw you leave here about ten minutes ago."

A chill ran up Mary's spine. Was Kari playing a joke? "I wasn't here half an hour ago," she told the nurse. "So, who fed my mother?"

Kari stared at her, then broke out into laughter. "You're messing with me, aren't you? I told you earlier that working the night shift creeped me out, so now you're having fun with me. Well, then, I'll play along. A woman who looked just like you and dressed like you came in earlier and fed Abby. So, now you're going to tell me it was a ghost, right? Or your doppelganger?" She laughed again. "That is funny."

Mary had no idea what was happening, but she didn't want to scare Kari. She smiled and forced out a laugh. "You caught me. Actually, I forgot my purse in the room, so I came back for it. I'll just check on my mom again and then head out."

"Okay," Kari said. "You have a great evening." The young nurse headed down the hallway.

Mary walked back into her mother's room. The TV was still playing *Friends,* but the sound was low. She looked down at her mother, and Abby stared back at her.

"I don't know who came and fed you tonight, Mom," Mary said. "But it had to have scared you. It wasn't me. Do you know who it was?"

Abby's eyes grew wider.

"Something strange is going on, and I have to get to the bottom of it," Mary said. "You should be okay tonight. And Judy will be here tomorrow at noon. I'll see you tomorrow night, okay?"

All Abby could do was stare at her. Mary never knew how

much her mom understood, but she knew for sure her mother realized that Mary wasn't the person here earlier.

So, who was it?

Mary left and headed to the parking lot. As soon as she got into her car and locked the doors, her phone buzzed. She lifted it out of her purse and hesitated. What if it was another text from the unknown person? Taking a breath, she tapped the text message, and it opened.

"Hope Mama enjoyed her meal tonight."

Mary's whole body shook. She dropped her phone into the cup holder and turned on the car. She had no idea who was doing this to her, but it was scaring her to death.

And from her mother's reaction, it was scaring her to death, too.

CHAPTER NINE

Mary had a restless night. She'd been so happy buying new clothes and looking forward to being a newer, better version of herself. But the stranger visiting her mother and the text message dragged her down.

She showered and fixed her hair, then added a little mascara and a nude lipstick to lift her spirits. Her new confidence was shattered last night by what happened. She decided to wear one of her older, boxier jackets over her new, slimmer dress pants with a new white sweater underneath. She didn't look completely different, but it was a start. And she wanted to wear her nicest suit tomorrow for Conrad's funeral.

Mary grabbed her Yeti tumbler and filled it with plain black coffee from her machine. After saying goodbye to Cassie, she headed out the door to work.

As she walked down the hallway toward her office, Janice practically jumped in front of her. "You look nice today," Janice said, smiling.

Compared to Janice, Mary felt like a slug, but she

appreciated the compliment. "Thanks. I went clothes shopping yesterday and found a few new suits."

Janice looked her up and down. "Love the pants and sweater, but isn't that your old blazer?"

"Yes. I guess I wasn't ready to change completely. I'm saving my new suit for tomorrow. Conrad's funeral is tomorrow afternoon."

"Oh, honey. I'm so sorry," Janice said. "Have they found his killer yet?"

Mary shook her head. "Not that I know of. Hopefully soon."

Janice gave her a little wave and headed toward the break room. Mary figured she was going to gossip to everyone in there.

Going into her office, Mary shut the door halfway and then sat at her desk. She had a lot of accounts to get through today, and since she was going to stretch out her lunch break, she knew she had to work fast.

Around noon, she slipped out of her office and out the back door. She was going to the hospital where she was born to ask a few questions. It took her half an hour to get to the hospital, which was in downtown St. Paul. She had to park in the parking ramp attached to the hospital. It was dark and echoed as her heels hit the ground, which freaked her out. Mary took the elevator downstairs to the reception desk and waited for her turn.

"Can I help you?" the receptionist behind the glass window asked.

"I hope so," Mary said. She pulled a file folder out of her big bag. "I was born in this hospital before the current hospital purchased it. I have my twin's birth certificate and death certificate here." She handed them to the woman. "I wondered if anyone still works here who might have information about the death of my sister."

Behind the receptionist was an older woman placing flower vases on a rolling cart. She glanced up and smiled at Mary, then returned to her work.

"I'm not sure how anyone here can help you," the receptionist said. "You have the documentation. What more do you need?"

"There's no cause of death listed on my sister's death certificate," Mary said. "I'd like to find the doctor to talk to him, although I assume he's retired."

"I can't give out that information," she said, handing the certificates back to Mary. "But let me call the Director of Nursing to see if she knows anything. What was your name?"

"It's Mary Westin. But I would have been born Mary James," Mary said.

A glass vase hit the floor and shattered behind the receptionist, making all three women jump.

"Colleen! Be careful!" the receptionist said, turning around. "There's glass everywhere."

Colleen looked down, then her face crumpled. "I'm so sorry. I'll get a broom and sweep it up."

The receptionist turned back to Mary, looking flustered. "Please have a seat in the waiting room, and I'll send the Director of Nursing right in."

"Thank you," Mary said. She wasn't sure how the Director of Nursing could help unless the woman had worked here thirty-six years ago. But Mary hadn't really expected anyone would be able to help her. She was grasping at straws.

Mary kept checking her watch as she waited. She should

have asked for an hour or two off to do this. Mr. Kerrigan will be angry if he comes looking for her and she's not at her desk.

Soon, a tall, middle-aged woman with dark hair approached Mary. "Are you Mary James?" she asked.

Mary stood. "Yes."

"I'm Dora Thompson, the Director of Nursing. What can I do for you?"

Mary explained her situation and that she was looking for any additional information about her twin.

"Oh, my," Dora said. "That was a while ago. This hospital took over the old one that used to be here. In fact, it was torn down, and this new structure was put up."

"But the records should still be here, shouldn't they?" Mary asked hopefully.

"Well, yes. Maybe. Although there's a storage facility where many of the older paper records are kept. And, you have the only two documents we'd have."

"Is there any chance of finding the doctor who signed the death certificate, or maybe a nurse who'd worked here then?" Mary asked. She was losing hope quickly.

"I've worked here for fifteen years, and I've never heard of that doctor," Dora said. "So, he must have retired years ago. And the chances of him remembering one birth out of thousands would be low."

Mary nodded. "I searched online and couldn't find him. I guess I was hoping for a miracle."

"Sorry," Dora said, standing. "I wish I could have helped you." She shook Mary's hand and headed back to her office.

Mary sighed and turned to leave. Suddenly, a hand touched her arm. She spun around and looked directly into the eyes of the woman who'd dropped the vase earlier.

"I'm sorry to startle you, dear," the woman said. "But I think I can help you. Can we go and talk somewhere?"

Mary stared at the woman. She looked to be in her sixties and had short gray hair and kind brown eyes. "Who are you?"

"I'm sorry. I'm Colleen Martin," the older woman said. "I was a nurse who assisted with births and worked in the nursery at the hospital long before this new one was built. I worked for the doctor on your sister's birth and death certificates."

"Really? That's amazing. Do you still work here?" Mary asked.

"Oh, no. I mean, I volunteer here now, but I retired a couple of years ago. But I'm sure I have the information you're seeking. Let's go to the hospital cafeteria, and we can talk."

Mary followed Colleen to the elevator, which took them to the second floor. They stepped out into a large room with dozens of tables on one side and counters to buy food on the other. Colleen led her to a table in the far corner where they would have privacy.

"Would you like coffee?" she asked Mary. "It's my treat. I get it for free." She chuckled.

"Yes, thank you," Mary said. She liked this petite older woman. She seemed nice.

"Here you are, dear," Colleen said. She sat opposite Mary and studied her for a moment. "My goodness, but you are the spitting image of her."

"Who?" Mary asked.

"Your twin sister," Colleen said.

Mary gasped. "What?"

"I'm sorry, dear. I should start at the beginning. I worked at the hospital the night you and your twin sister were born," Colleen said.

"Oh, my goodness! You were there? What happened? How did my sister die?" Mary had so many questions.

Colleen took a breath. "Let me explain, dear. I worked both days after you two were born. It was a tiny hospital then and not well funded. We mostly had low-income patients use our hospital in those days. Many never paid their bills. So, our hospital didn't have the best reputation. Anyway, both you and your sister were healthy and big for twins. You each were over six pounds. Your mother stayed longer than most because she'd bled a lot during the delivery."

Mary nodded. "Yes, my mom is a bleeder. Even a little cut will bleed for a long time."

"Well," Colleen continued. "Taking care of twins is a lot of work, so we generally brought in one baby at a time for the mother to feed. Your mom was bottle feeding, but even doing that with two babies is work. The day your sister died, I was the one who took you out of the room and brought in your sister. I usually give the mothers around twenty minutes to feed the baby, even though newborns don't eat much. It's really more for bonding."

Mary hung on her every word.

"When I returned to the room to bring your sister back to the nursery, your mother was sitting up in bed, staring down at the lifeless baby. She turned her head toward me and very calmly said, "The baby's dead.""

"Oh, my God!" Mary said, picturing the scene in her head. "How awful!"

"Yes, it was," Colleen said. "It was the juxtaposition of your mother's serene face and the horror of the baby dying. It was unreal. I'm sorry to say this to you, but what I saw in your mother's eyes scared me to death. But then her words were even worse. She shrugged and said, "We could only afford one anyway."

Mary was horrified. Judy had told her the exact same thing.

Colleen continued. "I snatched up the baby and ran to the nursery, where I gave the infant CPR. I was the only nurse on duty at the time, so I had no one to help me. The doctor had come in to deliver a baby and saw me trying to revive the infant. He was dumbstruck. He'd delivered the babies and knew they had been in excellent health."

"And?" Mary asked.

"I was able to bring the child back to life," Colleen said.

Mary's mouth dropped open. "So, my twin is alive?"

Colleen nodded. "What I'm about to tell you is only between you and me. I swear, if you tell anyone else, I'll deny ever saying this to you. I refuse to spend even a night in jail for what I did next."

Mary nodded. "I understand. But I need to know."

Colleen took a long sip of her coffee, then spoke again. "It was just me, the baby, and the doctor. I explained to him what had happened and what your mother had said to me. We both agreed there was something wrong with your mother, and that maybe she'd suffocated the child. There was no way I could give this baby back to her."

"You think my mother killed my twin?" Mary didn't like thinking that Abby was capable of that, but then again, she'd often thought her mother had pushed her father down the basement stairs.

"I'm sorry," Colleen said. "But I believed at the time your mother had tried to kill the baby. My husband and I had tried to have a baby for years, and here I was with a baby whose life I'd saved and whose mother may have hurt it. So, I told the doctor I wanted to keep the baby as my own."

"And he agreed?" Mary asked, stunned that a doctor would do that.

Colleen nodded. "We both knew the hospital couldn't afford any negative publicity if charges were brought against your mother. And we had no proof that your mother suffocated the child. But since she already thought the little girl was dead, we just did what we had to do. The doctor signed the death certificate and created a birth certificate that stated the baby girl was mine."

"So, she's alive? And you raised her?" Mary asked. "What about the grave? Did they bury an empty coffin?"

"Please don't hate me for this, but the doctor and I both knew of a newborn baby that was in the hospital morgue. The poor thing had been left in a garbage can to die. No one knew who the parents were. So, we tagged the baby as your sister, and that body was buried." Colleen looked down at her hands. "At the time, I thought it was the right thing to do. But as time passed, I realized I was paid back for my lies."

Mary leaned forward in her seat. "Why? What happened?"

"I took the baby home, and although my husband was stunned, he was also pleased. We had a baby. We told everyone we adopted the baby, and no one questioned it. We named her Allison Marie. At first, we were worried there might be brain damage from her having been suffocated, and we were prepared to care for her no matter what. But she met all the milestones and learned how to crawl, walk, and talk earlier than most babies. She seemed perfectly fine. Until she got older."

"I can't believe this," Mary said, still trying to digest Colleen's story. "You took my twin and raised her as your daughter. All these years, I had a sister and didn't know it."

"I'm sorry, dear. But what we did was for the child's own good. We also worried about your mother taking you home, too, but from what she'd said, she seemed willing to take home one baby. I'm sorry, but your mother was a terrible person."

"I can't argue with you about that," Mary told her. "My mother has done some terrible things." She looked up into the older woman's eyes. "What happened to my sister?"

"As I said," Colleen continued. "She was fine and thriving. But little things started happening, and then the incidents got worse. When she was five, she smashed a kitten's head with a big rock. She cried afterward, so I thought she was just too young to know what she was doing. Then, around twelve, her friend fell from a walking bridge that went over a freeway and broke her neck. Again, I thought it was an accident, but one of the other girls with them said she saw Allison push the girl over the side. No one could prove it, though, but I started to worry. Allison had those same dark eyes as your mother, and when I looked into them, all I saw was your mother saying the baby is dead. It was awful."

Colleen took a breath. "By the time Allison was fifteen, I knew she needed help. She was cruel one moment, sweet the next. I put her in therapy, but it didn't help. The therapist suggested having her treated at a behavioral hospital. It was hard to make her go, but I didn't know what else to do. Quite frankly, I was scared to death that she'd kill me and my husband in our sleep."

"Oh, my goodness," Mary said. "That's awful. But I understand the fear. My mother was always doing bizarre things that scared me and my older sister. Mental illness obviously runs in our family."

"That could be," Colleen said. "I always thought it was

the loss of oxygen Allison suffered, from being dead and then coming back to life. But if your mother was cruel too, it could be hereditary."

"Where is Allison now?" Mary asked.

"She stayed at the behavioral hospital until she was twenty-one, then was released. We took her back into our house, reluctantly. But she was able to get a job in a coffee shop near our home, and she seemed to be doing well. She even had a boyfriend, and when she was twenty-three, she moved in with him. I thought there was hope she'd live a normal life." Colleen stopped, her face looking sad. "But six months after moving in with her boyfriend, he was found dead in his car a few blocks from their apartment."

"Oh, no," Mary said.

"Allison claimed she knew nothing about what happened to the young man, but her DNA and fingerprints were all over him and the knife that killed him. The investigators found no one else's fingerprints or DNA on him. And there was blood in the apartment that she tried to clean up. Plus, the neighbor had heard them fighting loudly the night before. It was obvious she'd killed him."

Mary felt horrified. It was one thing to think a family member may have killed someone, but it was another to know for certain. She felt so bad for Colleen, who'd only wanted a child to love.

Colleen continued. "Allison wasn't fit to stand trial and was locked away in a secure treatment facility instead of a prison. She's still there today. I used to visit her often, but she made it clear that she hated me, so I stopped going. But I still put money in her account for incidentals and check up on her through the doctors. I hate to say it, but we're all safer with her locked up there."

"Oh, I'm so sorry," Mary said, reaching out and placing her hand over the older woman's hand. "This must be so hard on you and your husband."

"Sadly, my husband passed away two years ago. That's why I volunteer at the hospital. It's lonely being home with no one around."

"I'm so sorry," Mary said again. "But thank you for sharing your story with me. Now I know what happened to my twin sister. Even though you had problems with her, she was still better off with you as her mother. My mother would have found a way to get rid of her."

"Thank you, dear. I'm glad you aren't judging me too harshly."

Mary shook her head. "No. I wouldn't do that." She looked at her watch and realized she'd been there too long. Mr. Kerrigan will have a fit if he finds out she's been gone this long. "I have to get back to work. But thank you for the information. Can I ask which facility Allison is in?"

"Of course. "It's just north of here. I can map it for you on your phone."

Mary handed Colleen her phone, and she typed in the name and town. "I'm going to give you my number and address as well. Just in case you need to contact me."

"Thank you, Colleen," Mary said, standing. The older woman also stood, and Mary hugged her. She felt like she'd known this woman her entire life.

"Take care of yourself, dear," Colleen said. They parted at the elevators. Colleen needed to go downstairs while Mary had to go upstairs to the parking garage.

As Mary drove back to work, Colleen's story filled her

thoughts. It was unbelievable. But Mary had no doubt in her mind that her mother was capable of killing a baby. The fact that Allison then became a killer wasn't surprising either. She wished things had been different and she'd grown up with her twin sister. But it would have been a nightmare living with her, too.

Mary's exit appeared, and she looked in her rear-view mirror to change lanes. Flipping on the blinker to go right, she turned her head to make sure no cars were in the lane beside her. Suddenly, a black Ford Escape pulled up beside her, and the woman stared right at her.

Mary gasped as she looked directly at her twin.

CHAPTER TEN

Mary's heart beat faster as she stared at the woman in the car. Then the car sped up and passed her, heading for the off-ramp. Mary followed her and exited the freeway, too. But when she got to the stoplight at the cross street, the black car was nowhere to be found.

Had she imagined it? Had she seen her reflection in the car window?

"No!" Mary said aloud. "There was a woman, and she looked just like me. But how?"

Feeling unnerved, she drove back to work and took several deep breaths before leaving her car and going inside. Mary was almost to her office when Mr. Kerrigan approached her, his expression angry.

"Since when are you allowed to take two-hour lunch breaks?" he yelled at Mary.

"I'm so sorry, Mr. Kerrigan," Mary said. She felt the eyes of the entire office on her. She needed a good lie fast. "My appointment went longer than I thought it would."

"What appointment?" he bellowed.

"Um," Mary glanced around nervously. "I had a doctor's appointment today. I was sure I'd be there and back within the hour, but the doctor was running late."

Mr. Kerrigan stood there for a moment, staring at her.

Mary knew he was weighing his options. He'd look like an idiot if he yelled at her about a doctor's appointment, but he was still angry.

"From now on, I want to know if you'll be late. Do you understand?" Mr. Kerrigan said, lowering his voice.

"Yes, sir," Mary said softly. She quickly ducked into her office to hide from all the prying eyes.

Janice poked her head inside and smiled at Mary. "Ignore that old windbag," she said. "I don't know why he acts that way. Is everything okay with you?"

Mary nodded. "I'm fine."

"Great. Do you want me to get you coffee? What type do you like?" Janice asked.

Mary was on the verge of tears after being yelled at by Mr. Kerrigan. And now, here was Janice, being nice to her. "Thank you. That would be so nice." She told Janice what she liked, and she left to get her coffee.

Mary worked the rest of the afternoon, never leaving her desk. She hadn't eaten lunch earlier, so she was starving. But she didn't dare go out to grab something and bring it back to her desk.

It was hard to concentrate on work with all that she'd learned today. Her twin sister was alive and living in a treatment facility not far away. That was difficult to wrap her head around. She wanted to tell Ginny what Colleen had revealed, but she didn't dare get caught on a personal call right now.

She'd just have to wait until tonight.

At four forty-five, Mary cleaned off her desk and was about to turn off her computer when Mr. Kerrigan came into her office.

"These files need to be updated by nine tomorrow morning," he said brusquely, tossing four folders on her desk.

Mary looked from the files back up to her boss. "I was just getting ready to leave."

He stared down at her. "Oh, were you? You took a two-hour lunch break, and now you want to leave? Just get them done. I want them on my desk first thing in the morning." He stormed out of her office.

Mary held back tears as she looked through the files. He did this on purpose. Why was he so mean to her? All she'd ever done was make him look good to his clients.

Turning back to her computer, she opened the first account that needed updating. This was going to take her at least an hour or more. There was no way she'd make it to the nursing home to feed her mother.

Mary called the nursing home and explained she wouldn't be there to help her mother. The receptionist said her mother would be fine and one of the nurses would help her with her meal.

Feeling guilty, Mary started working on the files.

Mary got up once to go to the ladies' room down the hall. The entire place was quiet. She was the only one working late. Well, except for Mr. Kerrigan. Across the room, she saw a light on in his office through the frosted glass window on his door.

"I don't know what he's working on," she mumbled to herself. "He doesn't do any of this work."

She returned to her office and shut the door. Being alone in the building at night frightened her.

The work took longer than she'd anticipated, and Mary didn't finish until six thirty. Sighing, she piled the folders together with the updated printed sheets in them and walked into the office area. She crossed the large room filled with walled-off cubicles to get to Mr. Kerrigan's door. The light was still on in his office, but she didn't want to see him, so she placed the files in the plastic file holder on his door and headed across the room again. Grabbing her purse, she left out the back door at six forty-five and got in her car.

It was useless to go to her mother's nursing home now since they would have already given her the sleeping medicine. So, Mary turned her car in the direction of her house.

Mary was relieved to finally pull into her driveway. She'd had such an emotional day, and being yelled at in front of everyone at work hadn't helped her frame of mind. She changed into comfy clothes and fed Cassie, then made herself a sandwich. She was past hungry at this point, but she knew she had to eat.

As she sat at her kitchen counter, Mary hit Ginny's name on her phone. Her sister answered after three rings.

"Wow. Another call from you," Ginny teased.

"Sorry to bother you," Mary said. "But I learned something interesting that I know you'd want to hear about."

"Okay."

Ginny sounded like she was talking in a tunnel. "Why is it so loud around you?"

"Oh. I'm in my car. Trevor forgot to tell me it's his turn to take snacks to soccer practice after school tomorrow, so I'm on my way to the grocery store. Kids!"

"You're lucky to have them, no matter how much work they are," Mary said. She'd love to be married with children.

"I learned today that my twin sister didn't die. She's alive and was adopted by a woman who worked at the hospital where we were born."

"Are you kidding me?" Ginny sounded shocked. "How is that possible?"

Mary quickly told Ginny the story. When she finished, Ginny said, "It wouldn't surprise me if Mom suffocated the child. It's crazy what that woman is capable of."

"I know," Mary said. "But the weird thing is, even though my twin is supposed to be locked away in a treatment facility, I keep seeing someone who looks exactly like me following me around. It's scary."

"I'm sure you're just imagining it," Ginny said dismissively. "You've always been afraid of the dark and being alone. You're probably just seeing your reflection."

"It's not my imagination," Mary insisted. "I'm also getting strange texts from someone. Is that my imagination, too?"

"Well, just block them," Ginny said offhandedly. "Listen. I'm at the grocery store now. Thanks for filling me in on all the freaky twin sister stuff. Keep me updated if you learn anything else. I've got to go."

Mary said goodbye and hit the end button on her phone. She was surprised that Ginny wasn't as excited about her twin being alive as she was. But then, Ginny had a busy life, so she supposed she had a lot more on her mind.

"Okay, Cassie," she said to her cat, who'd finished her meal on the counter. "Tomorrow is another long day with Conrad's funeral. I'm sure Mr. Kerrigan will have a coronary when I tell him I need to leave early for it." She put everything away and headed to her bedroom at the back of the house. Her phone buzzed, and she glanced down at it. Someone had sent her a text. She swiped it and froze when she saw the message.

"I took care of your problem. You're welcome."

Mary stared at the message and thought, what problem?

* * *

Mary didn't sleep well after the creepy text message and was exhausted when her alarm went off.

After showering, Mary spent more time than usual fixing her hair and applied a little makeup. She'd never been one to wear makeup, but she liked how mascara made her eyes stand out and lipstick gave her a finished look. It gave her confidence, something she desperately needed.

Next, she put on one of her new outfits. She wore the pinstripe skirt with the black and white blouse and the solid black jacket. Next, she slipped on the black leather heels. Looking in the full-length mirror, she was stunned by her reflection. Was that really her? She actually had a figure wearing the fitted clothing and looked just as nice as Janice.

Well, almost.

She fed Cassie and then filled her tumbler with coffee. "Well, here I go, Cassie. Let's hope no one makes fun of me."

The cat only stared at her.

Once at work, Mary walked through the back door and down the hallway to her office. Many of her co-workers turned and stared as she walked by. Some smiled and said good morning. Janice came right up to her and said, "Wow, Mary. You look amazing!"

Mary felt a blush warm her cheeks. She wasn't used to

positive attention. "Thanks, Janice. You always look great. I thought it was time to try to dress nicer."

"Well, you're killing it, girl," Janice said. "Keep it up!"

Mary walked a little taller into her office. For the first time in her life, she felt like she fit in.

Before starting work, Mary gathered all her courage and emailed Mr. Kerrigan about her needing to leave at two-thirty to attend a funeral. As she worked, she waited for him to storm into her office and yell at her. Around ten-thirty, Janice poked her head inside Mary's office and asked, "Did Randall tell you he was taking today off?"

"No," Mary said, surprised. "Isn't he here?"

Janice shook her head. "He had a nine o'clock meeting scheduled but wasn't here for it. There's another man here for a meeting, too. And his door is locked."

Mary stood. "Really? He had me work late last night so he'd be ready for those meetings. I put the folders in the holder on his door before I left last night."

"Let's see if they're still in there," Janice said. The two women walked between the cubicles in the middle to Kerrigan's office door. The folders Mary had placed there the night before were still there.

"His light was on in the office when I left last night," Mary said. "Can you tell if it's still on?"

Janice shook her head. "I think we'd better ask Mr. Clark to unlock his door. Only the partners have keys for each other's doors." Janice walked over to Mr. Clark's office, and a minute later, he came out with his keys in hand.

"I'm sure Randall is just sick or something," Mr. Clark said. "But he should have rescheduled his meetings."

Mary had never known Mr. Kerrigan to miss a meeting.

He was a workaholic.

Mr. Clark opened the door, and he and Janice stepped inside. Janice screamed.

* * *

An hour later, the accounting office was swarming with police. Janice was still shaking and crying in Mary's office. Mary sat with her arm around her, but Janice couldn't be pacified.

"It was awful!" she kept saying. "There was so much blood."

Mr. Kerrigan was found on the floor behind his desk with his 14K gold letter opener stabbed through his neck.

A police officer stepped into Mary's office. "I'm sorry, but I need to get a statement from both of you ladies," he said.

"Of course," Mary said. "Janice was the one who found Mr. Kerrigan. Do you want me to step outside while she talks to you?"

"That's not necessary," the officer said. He leaned against Mary's desk and opened his little notepad. "Can I have your full name, please?" he asked, staring at Janice.

"Janice Wilton," she said between sniffles.

"And how long have you worked here?"

"About six years."

"Can you tell me what your position here is?" the officer asked.

"I'm a staff accountant for Mr. Clark," Janice said.

The officer looked up. "If you work for Mr. Clark, why were you the one who discovered Mr. Kerrigan?"

Janice clutched the handful of tissues Mary had given her. "I noticed Randall had appointments and wasn't here, and his door was locked. So, that's why I asked Mr. Clark to open

Randall's door to check on him."

"Can you tell me what you saw?" the officer asked.

"Nothing at first. His light was on, and his desk chair was pushed back. I walked around his desk, and that's when I saw him. He was lying in a pool of blood, his eyes wide open." Janice started crying again. "It was horrific."

"I'm sorry to have to put you through this, Ms. Wilton," the officer said. "Did you notice anything else?"

She nodded. "Yes. Something shiny and gold was stuck in his neck."

The officer nodded. "How well did you know Mr. Kerrigan?"

She stared at him with wide eyes. "Not that well. I mean, I've worked here a while, so we've talked in passing in the hallway. That's about it."

"Thank you, Ms. Wilton." The officer's eyes turned to Mary. "And what is your name and position here?"

"I'm Mary Westin," Mary said. "And I work as a staff accountant for Mr. Kerrigan."

"I see," the officer said. "So, you worked directly with Mr. Kerrigan?"

"Yes. I've worked here for twelve years."

The officer studied Mary for a moment. "I noticed you call him Mr. Kerrigan, but Ms. Wilton called him by his first name. Aren't you on a first-name basis with your boss?"

Mary shook her head. "No. We had a very professional working relationship. He never asked me to call him by his first name."

"Randall was awful to Mary," Janice piped up. "He was always yelling at her and making her work late. Just yesterday, he yelled at her in front of the entire office. It was terrible."

Mary frowned at Janice. She wasn't helping. "It wasn't so

bad," Mary said. "Mr. Kerrigan is a busy man and sometimes gets stressed."

"Didn't he make you work late last night?" Janice asked, looking at Mary. "Goodness. You could have been here when he was murdered!"

"Were you here last night?" the officer asked, looking interested.

Mary couldn't believe Janice had said all of that. Did she want her to be arrested? "Yes, I was, but I had closed my door and never heard anything strange. I worked until six-thirty, and then I left by six forty-five."

"Hm." The officer wrote something in his notebook. "Which door did you leave from last night?"

"The back door," Mary said. "I always park in the back like everyone else."

"Okay. How is it you remember the exact time you left?" he asked her.

"Because I usually help my mother at the nursing home right after work, and I missed going there because I stayed here," Mary said. "She's usually asleep by six or six-thirty because they give her a sedative each night. I looked at the time and realized it was too late for me to go see her."

The officer looked at Mary for a moment, as if he were comparing the fact that she visited her mother at a nursing home each night against the fact that she could have killed Kerrigan.

"That's all I need right now," he said, standing. "But please stay in your offices until we get the all-clear. Someone else may have questions for you."

"Thank you, Officer," Mary said as he left the room.

At this point, Janice had stopped crying. "I'd better go

to my cubicle," she said, standing. She went to the door, then turned. "Isn't it weird? First, your husband was murdered, and now Randall. Doesn't that creep you out?"

Mary took a breath, not sure how to respond. When she didn't answer, Janice turned and left her office.

Mary hoped the police didn't think to put the two murders together.

She sat at her desk, but didn't feel like working. Her mind was jumbled. Had she been here when Mr. Kerrigan was murdered last night? That thought gave her chills.

Mary stood again and walked down to the coffee room. She hoped they'd allow her to make a cup of coffee. But when she got there, she ran right into Detective Hodges.

"Hello, Mary," the detective said. "I was just coming to your office."

Mary's heart pounded. The only reason he'd be here is because he'd tied both cases together.

"I'd like to speak with you in private. But not here. Let's go down to the station," Detective Hodges said.

Oh, my God! Was she under arrest?

CHAPTER ELEVEN

Mary stood there, frightened. "Am I under arrest?"

Detective Hodges chuckled. "No. Not at all," he said kindly. "But I'd like to talk to you without so many ears around. Why don't I drive you there?"

"Can't I drive myself?" she asked.

"I'd rather drive you," he said. "You seem a little out of sorts."

Mary glanced around and noticed that some of her co-workers were watching them. She didn't need more people thinking she'd killed Mr. Kerrigan. "Okay. I'll get my purse." She tried not to run to her office. Her adrenaline was pumping fast, and she didn't want to look like she'd lost it entirely.

Mary pulled her purse from her desk drawer and clicked off her computer. When she turned to leave, Detective Hodges was standing in her office doorway.

"Wow. They sure don't give you much space around here, do they?"

"It's all I need to work in," Mary said. "And it's more private than the cubicles on the main office floor."

The detective turned and studied the area. "Is that Mr. Kerrigan's office straight across from here?"

Mary came up behind him. "Yes. The partners each have big offices in the front."

"Hm." Detective Hodges sounded thoughtful. He turned back to Mary. "Shall we go?"

Mary nodded. As they walked down the hallway toward the back door, she felt like she was being led to the gallows. Everyone in the office was staring and whispering.

The drive to the station was quiet, and then Detective Hodges led Mary to a small room with a table and chairs. "Do you want anything to eat or drink?" he asked. "I have to check on something, and then we can talk."

"Water would be nice," she said, feeling uncomfortable in the room. It was so plain, like a cell.

He smiled. "I'll send someone in with it." He left, shutting the door behind him.

Mary stared at the door, wondering if he'd locked it.

A few minutes later, a female officer came in with a bottle of water. "We'll be ordering lunch soon. Would you like us to order you something?"

"Will I be here that long?" Mary asked, growing anxious again.

She smiled. "Detective Hodges said he might be a while. How about a sandwich or a salad?"

"A salad would be nice, thank you," Mary said. The officer nodded and left.

As Mary sat in the small room, her mind was spinning. Who killed Mr. Kerrigan? He was uptight and mean sometimes, but never once had she thought life would be better if he were dead. And why would anyone think she was capable of killing him or Conrad? All she'd ever done was work hard and help others.

Then she remembered the text message she received the night before.

Mary pulled her phone out of her purse and stared at the message.

"I took care of your problem. You're welcome."

The message gave her chills all over again. Did the sender kill Mr. Kerrigan?

Mary wasn't sure what to do. If she showed Detective Hodges the texts she'd been getting, he might believe she was conspiring with the texter to kill people. On the other hand, telling the detective she's being followed and getting weird texts might help him find the real murderer.

She didn't know what to do, and it scared her.

Half an hour later, Mary was still waiting. Her salad had arrived, and she tried to eat a few bites. It was getting late, and she'd need to leave to attend Conrad's funeral soon. If she didn't try to eat more now, she'd pass out from hunger later.

Finally, an hour and a half after leaving her in the room, Detective Hodges returned, carrying a laptop computer.

"I'm sorry for making you wait so long," he said immediately. "I'm glad to see they brought you food and a drink."

Mary nodded. She was on edge and afraid to say anything.

"I was waiting on some evidence from the crime scene before I spoke to you," Hodges continued. "I think you'll find it as interesting as I did."

"Do I need a lawyer?" Mary blurted out. With all the time

she'd had to think, her nerves were frayed.

Detective Hodges looked surprised. "No, not at all, unless you feel it's necessary."

"I don't want to end up charged with something I didn't do," Mary told him. "So, if you think I need a lawyer, please tell me."

Detective Hodges smiled and shook his head. "No, Mary. You don't need a lawyer. And I promise if something happens and I think you do, I'll tell you immediately.

Mary took a deep breath. "Okay." Her voice was shaky.

Detective Hodges studied her for a moment, then leaned toward her. "Okay. I'm not supposed to tell you this, but we didn't find your fingerprints anywhere in Mr. Westin's apartment. The fingerprints we found on the murder weapon haven't been matched to anyone yet. But you're in the clear. The DNA matches haven't come back yet, but I honestly don't believe your DNA will be found on or near Mr. Westin's body. Does that make you feel better?"

A long sigh escaped Mary. "I'm not a suspect?"

He shook his head. "No. But the reason they called me in for Kerrigan's murder is because you work there. It seemed like too much of a coincidence that you knew both murder victims."

Mary tensed again. "I didn't kill Mr. Kerrigan, I swear."

"I believe you, Mary," Hodges said. "But we have some strange evidence I want to show you." He opened the laptop and turned it on. Then, he opened a video file. "I understand you were in the office last night until around six forty-five, right?"

"Yes. I left about that time."

"Okay. This video from outside your building shows you

leaving close to that time and getting into your car," Hodges said. "Here. Watch." He turned on the video, and in black and white, Mary could be seen leaving the building, getting inside her car, and driving away.

"That proves I left then, right?" Mary asked.

"Yes," Hodges said. "But we don't have an official time of death yet for Kerrigan. Now, I want to show you another video." He clicked on another file and opened it. A person dressed exactly like Mary ran out the front door of the accounting office at six-fifteen, got into a black car, and drove away.

Mary frowned. "That was at six-fifteen?"

"Yes."

"But I was in my office at six-fifteen. I worked until around six-thirty, then I went to Mr. Kerrigan's office and slipped the file folders into the box on his door, then returned to my office to get ready to leave."

"Did you hear anything strange while you were working?"

"No. I had my door shut, so I didn't see or hear anything."

Detective Hodges sat back in his chair. "Mary. Were you the one who ran out the front door and into the car at six-fifteen?"

Mary lifted her eyes to his. "No. I never park in front. And you saw me leaving at six forty-five. I don't even have a key for the front or back doors. So, if I leave, I can't get back inside."

"Then who was able to get inside the building after closing time, kill Kerrigan, then leave out the front door? And why is she dressed like you?" Hodges asked.

"I don't know," Mary said, feeling defeated. "But it wasn't me."

Hodges sighed. "Well, unless you have an evil twin I don't know about, then we've got to figure out who's running around killing people while dressing like you."

Mary's heart sank. Little did Detective Hodges know, but she did have an evil twin, except she was locked up in a treatment facility.

"Unfortunately, we couldn't get a license plate number from the video," Hodges continued.

"You don't see the face in the video either," Mary offered. "Or in the video you found near Conrad's apartment. There's no real proof it's me."

"You're right about that," Hodges said. "Unfortunately, prosecutors have charged people with much less evidence. And today, it seemed like your co-workers all wanted to throw you under the bus. Several said that Kerrigan yelled at you in the office yesterday. And others mentioned he made you work late quite often. One person said it was like Kerrigan was trying to get you to quit."

"He wasn't nice to me sometimes, but he knew I was a hard worker. I think he just didn't like me. I'm not sexy or pretty like the other women who work in the office," Mary said.

Hodges frowned. "Then the guy was blind."

Mary looked up quickly. Was that a compliment?

"Am I being charged with something, or am I free to go?" Mary asked. She was so tired after all of this. It was mentally draining. "If I leave now, I can still attend Conrad's funeral."

"Oh, that's right," Detective Hodges said. "I can drive you there since I'm going, too. Then I'll drop you at your car."

"So, I'm free to go?" Mary asked again.

"Of course. I have no proof you killed your boss. But I suggest you don't try to leave the country. That will make you look guilty." He grinned.

"Okay," Mary said seriously.

Detective Hodges laughed. "That was a joke."

"Oh, yeah. I guess I'm not in a joking kind of mindset."

"No. I suppose not. Sorry," Detective Hodges said. He stood. "Come on. I'll drive you to the church."

They were silent in his car on the way to the church. Once there, Mary chose to sit in the back, and Hodges sat next to her. The service was just beginning, and they didn't want to disrupt it.

Mary saw Conrad's parents in the front row along with his brother, Tom, and his family. Conrad's girlfriend, Marissa, sat with them. Even though Mary didn't know Ida and Grant Westin very well because they lived in Florida, she felt bad for them. Losing a child had to be devastating.

After the service, Mary motioned to Hodges to leave before the casket came down the aisle. They slipped out and walked to his car.

"I really don't want to talk to the family," Mary said. "I barely know them, and I'm afraid they might think I killed Conrad."

"Nothing about you has been shared with them or the news," Detective Hodges said. "They have no idea who killed their son."

"That's good to know. Maybe we should drive to the cemetery and attend that service before we leave," Mary suggested. "There will be fewer people there in case they're angry with me."

"Sure." They got inside his black SUV and headed for the cemetery. They arrived before the funeral procession, so they stayed in the car to wait.

"Thank you for driving me today," Mary said. "I was so upset this morning; it wouldn't have been a good idea for me to be driving."

He nodded. "I figured that you were. You seemed shaken up by your boss's death. I kind of figured if you'd killed him, you would have been happy to see him dead."

She turned and looked at him. His blue eyes were twinkling, so she figured he was teasing her. "You joke a lot for a homicide detective."

This made him laugh. "What I do is so serious, if I didn't joke occasionally, it would drive me crazy."

She smiled. "I suppose that's true. It must be a hard job mentally. I bet you don't see the good in many humans."

"Oh, it's not that bad. I see a lot of terrible things, but I know there are good people out there," Hodges said.

"Do you think I'm one of the terrible people or good people?" Mary asked. She didn't know why she'd asked, but she really didn't want Hodges to think she was a murderer.

He studied her. "At first glance, I'd say you're an ordinary person who just wants to work and make a good life for herself. And you have to be kind and generous with all you do for your disabled mother. But then again, I also see that there's more to you than even you know."

Mary's brows rose. "Is that a good thing?"

"I think so."

The hearse had parked, and a group of people were gathering at the graveside. Detective Hodges and Mary exited the car and joined the group. After the minister said his last prayer, Mary turned to Hodges to tell him they should leave. But before she opened her mouth, a woman's voice yelled sharply at her.

"What are you doing here?"

Mary looked up and saw Marissa Craig coming toward her, teetering on her spiky high heels.

"You don't belong here!" she yelled. "Conrad wouldn't want you here."

Conrad's brother, Tom, came hurrying behind Marissa.

"We should go," Mary said, turning, but Marissa caught up to her and grabbed her arm. Mary was pulled around and found herself looking into green eyes spitting fire at her.

"You shouldn't be here," Marissa yelled. "You killed Conrad. I know you did."

"Hey, wait, Marissa," Tom said, catching up to them. "You can't go around calling people killers. There's no evidence yet on who killed my brother."

"She did! I know she did." Marissa spat. "She owed Conrad money and didn't want to pay him."

Tom sighed. He glanced up and noticed Detective Hodges for the first time. "Detective. Did you bring Mary?"

Detective Hodges nodded. "It's nice to see you again, Mr. Westin. Yes. I escorted her here. She didn't mean to cause any problems. We were just leaving."

By now, Conrad's parents, Ida and Grant, had approached the group. "What is all the fuss, Marissa?" Grant asked, sounding annoyed. His eyes landed on Mary, and he smiled. "Mary. I'm so glad you made it to Conrad's funeral. He'd be happy to see you here."

Mary thought she was going to cry. Both Grant and Ida stepped up to hug her. Clearly, they didn't believe she'd killed their son.

"I'm sorry we didn't call you sooner," Ida said. "You should have been sitting with our family. After all, you two were married."

"How can you say that?" Marissa said. "She's the one who killed him."

"Marissa, that's enough," Grant said sternly. "We've known Mary much longer than we've known you, and we know she's not a killer."

Marissa's face turned red. She spun on her heel, leaving a deep divot in someone's grave, and stormed off.

"That girl," Grant said, shaking his head. He smiled at Mary. "We're having a reception at Tom's house. You're welcome to join us."

"Thank you," Mary said, relieved they still cared about her. "But it's getting late, and I have to go check on my mother at the nursing home.

Ida and Grant both nodded. "Well, you take care of yourself, dear. And ignore Marissa. She was always jealous of your relationship with Conrad." They nodded to the detective and all three of them walked away.

"See. Not everyone thinks you're a murderer," Detective Hodges said.

Mary gave him side eye. "Thanks."

They both turned to walk to his car, and Mary gazed out over the cemetery. A woman wearing a baggy black suit stood by a small black car. Mary stopped and stared. The woman looked just like her. It was her double, staring back at her.

CHAPTER TWELVE

Mary took off at a run as fast as her heels would allow. Damn, she wished she hadn't worn heels. She needed to catch the woman and finally learn the truth of who she was.

"Mary! Wait!" Detective Hodges ran after her. "Where are you going?"

Mary was too late. The woman hopped into her car and sped off before she could reach her. Mary wasn't able to get her license plate number, either.

Detective Hodges caught up to her. "Where were you going?" he asked, breathing hard.

"I saw her! I saw a woman dressed in clothes like mine and she looked like me," Mary said, between breaths. "But I couldn't catch her or even get her license plate number."

The detective stared at her strangely. "You saw someone impersonating you?"

"Yes! Just like in the video you have from last night. She was wearing the same baggy suit like I used to wear, and she had brown hair. Didn't you see her get into that small black car?"

"No. I was paying more attention to where you were running off to," Hodges said.

Mary was frustrated. She knew the woman wasn't a reflection or a figment of her imagination this time. She'd seen her.

"Are you okay?" Detective Hodges asked. "It's been a long, trying day."

"I saw her," Mary mumbled. Should she tell the detective about the sightings of her double and the texts? Or would he think she was crazy? She decided to keep it all to herself. It did sound like she was going insane.

"I need to get back to my car," Mary said, turning to walk toward Hodges' car. "I have to check in on my mother."

"Okay." They walked together in silence, and then he drove her back to the accounting office.

"Your office will be closed tomorrow so they can work on the crime scene," Hodges told her. "You won't have to go in until Thursday."

"Okay," Mary said, feeling defeated. "Thanks for the ride."

Hodges leaned toward the passenger door as she got out. "Are you sure you're okay? Do you want me to make sure you get home safely tonight?"

"No," Mary said. "I'm fine. I have to go to the nursing home first, and then I'll be going home."

"I can follow you. It's no problem."

Mary smiled. "You're relentless. Go home and have dinner. I'll be fine, I promise."

He waited until she got into her car, then waved and drove off. Mary headed to her mother's care facility.

"Hi, Mary. You're early tonight," the receptionist said when Mary entered the building.

"Yeah. I've been running around a lot today."

"I love your suit. Classy," she told Mary.

"Thanks." That was the nicest thing anyone had told her today.

When she arrived in her mother's room, the TV was turned down low, and her mother was sleeping. Her dinner tray wouldn't come for another half an hour, so Mary sat in the chair near the bed and watched the old sitcom on television.

She was exhausted. Detective Hodges was right; it had been a trying day. When Marissa had run up to her yelling, she thought for sure she'd cause a scene. Luckily, Conrad's parents didn't think Mary had done anything wrong. And it looked like they didn't have much patience for Marissa, either. Hopefully, Mary will be cleared of both murders very soon. Despite what Detective Hodges said, she knew the police were checking her DNA and fingerprints in Mr. Kerrigan's office. She was definitely a suspect.

Mary turned toward her mother and saw that her eyes were open. She stood and hit the floor pedal to raise the head of the bed. "It's just me, Mom," Mary said. "I'm here to feed you dinner. I'm sure they will bring it in soon."

Her mother stared at her with wide eyes.

"It really is me this time, Mom. I don't know who came here the other day, but I know it scared you. Whoever is running around impersonating me is scaring me as well." Mary thought for a moment, then decided she needed to confront her mother. "Mom. I know I had a twin when I was born, even though you never told me. And I know that after she died in the hospital, she was resuscitated by the nurse. Did you know my twin was still alive?"

Abby's eyes widened. From the look of surprise on her face, Mary concluded her mother hadn't known.

"The nurse made an agreement with the doctor to take the baby as her own. She thought you had purposely suffocated my twin. Did you? Did you try to kill my twin sister?" Mary asked.

Of course, there was no way for Abby to respond. And Mary didn't know if her mother understood a word she'd said.

"Well, if you did, then you didn't succeed," Mary said. "My twin is in a treatment facility for killing someone. She's mentally ill and needs to be watched over. But it's kind of creepy because someone is following me around, impersonating me. I have no idea who."

There was a knock on the door, and then Amy brought in Abby's food tray. "You look nice today," Amy said, smiling at Mary. "Special occasion?"

"I went to my ex-husband's funeral today," Mary said.

"Oh, my. I had no idea. Did anyone give you any trouble?"

"Not really," Mary said. "Conrad's parents were as nice as can be. Conrad's girlfriend, though, was a jerk, but everyone calmed her down."

Amy shook her head. "Such a shame for a young man like that to lose his life. Did you see the evening news? There was another murder not far from here. At some office, I think. Since when is our little suburb so dangerous?"

"That was at the accounting office where I work," Mary said. "My boss was killed last night."

Amy frowned. "Weren't you working late last night? I fed your mother her dinner because the receptionist said you were being held up at work."

Mary nodded. "I was. But I never heard anything, so it might have happened after I left."

"My goodness. How scary is that? You'd better watch out for yourself, dear. Being a single female and living alone makes you a target."

That comment didn't make Mary feel any safer.

Mary fed her mother, even though Abby didn't eat very much. Then she told her mother she'd be back again the next evening. On the way out, she told the receptionist she was done.

"Thanks, Mary. I'll tell Amy to collect the tray."

As Mary walked out to her car, her phone buzzed. She was afraid to look at it. She wasn't sure if she could handle another creepy message. But when she finally forced herself to look at it, she saw it was from Detective Hodges.

"I have a few more questions. Do you want to meet some-where, or should I bring a pizza to your house and we'll share it?"

Mary wondered if this was an interrogation or a dinner date. A dinner date wouldn't be so bad. Detective Hodges was a nice-looking man. No, like he said, he just had a few more questions.

"Bring pizza," she texted. *"I'll be home in a few minutes."*

He gave her a thumbs-up. Yep. Definitely not a dinner date.

As soon as Mary got home, she quickly changed into one of her new sweaters and a pair of jeans. She'd been wearing the suit all day and wanted to be comfortable. By the time she'd fed Cassie, the doorbell rang. Taking a breath to calm herself, Mary opened the door.

"Hi. I hope you like pepperoni pizza. I thought it was the safest choice," Detective Hodges said.

Mary already knew the detective was handsome, but dressed in jeans and a white shirt, he looked amazing. She forced herself not to stare. "It's fine," she said, leading him to the kitchen table.

"Well, who's this?" Hodges asked, stopping to pet Cassie, who was eating on the kitchen counter.

"That's Cassie. Sorry, she's on the counter. I know it's not sanitary, but it's easier to feed her up there," Mary said.

"Doesn't bother me," Hodges said. "You'd be surprised what my dog gets away with."

"You have a dog?" Mary was surprised. "Don't you work too many hours to have one?"

"We manage," he said, smiling. "He's a Siberian Husky named Riley. He keeps me company." He placed the pizza box on the table.

"I'm afraid all I have is soda or water," Mary said. "I don't usually keep wine or beer around."

"That's fine. I'll have a soda."

She brought out plates and napkins, then poured soda into glasses with ice. When they sat down, she chose to sit across the table from him.

"Do you always bring dinner to your murder suspects?" Mary asked, teasing.

"You're not a murder suspect, Mary," he said seriously. "Not yet, at least."

That didn't make her feel any more hopeful.

"How well do you know Conrad's girlfriend, Marissa?" Hodges asked. "She seemed like a loose cannon."

"I don't know her at all. She works at the dealership where Conrad worked. She's the reason he left me. Well, besides the fact that I was always working or helping my mother," Mary said. She took a bite of pizza and sighed.

Hodges chuckled. "Is the pizza good?"

"Yes. It's so good. I usually eat frozen diet meals. This tastes great."

"How long were you and Conrad divorced?"

"We separated about a year and a half ago, but we've been divorced for a year," Mary said.

"Then why didn't Marissa and Conrad live together?" Hodges asked.

Mary shrugged. "I never asked, but I wondered the same thing. When Conrad moved into his apartment, I thought she'd move in, too. But she never did." She looked up at Hodges. "Why? Is she a suspect?"

"Everyone's a suspect until we can rule them out," Hodges said. "But like I told you, we didn't find any evidence you were ever in his apartment, so you're pretty much cleared."

Mary let out a sigh. "That's a relief."

"Of course, the fact that your boss is dead doesn't look good," Hodges said.

"I didn't kill Mr. Kerrigan."

He nodded. "I don't believe you did. But we'll follow the evidence on that one, too."

They finished eating, and Mary put the dishes in the dishwasher. "Thanks for bringing pizza. It was nice not eating alone for a change."

"You're welcome," he said. He was still sitting at the table, watching her with those bright blue eyes.

"Do you have any more questions?" Mary asked.

"No. Not really. We can talk after they finish processing the scene at your work." Hodges stood, took his glass to the sink, rinsed it out, and set it in the dishwasher.

"Wow. Someone trained you well," Mary said without thinking. The minute the words left her lips, she regretted them.

"My mother trained me well," he said, smiling. "With it

being just me and my dog, I've learned to take care of myself."

"Good to know," Mary said, smiling.

"Thanks for letting me come over," Hodges said. "I get tired of eating alone, too." He headed for the front door.

"Is that the only reason you came over?" Mary asked, following him to the door. "Just to ask me questions?" She knew she should just let him go, but it did seem odd that he'd want to come to her house.

"Can I be completely honest?" Hodges said.

"Yes."

"I wanted to get to know you better. You seem like such a nice person, and you've been caught up in all this mess. Sorry if I made you feel uncomfortable."

"Oh, no. You didn't," Mary said quickly. "I like your company."

He smiled, and Mary felt herself blush.

Mary's phone rang and she pulled it out of her pocket. It was Renee Wheatin, who lived next door to her mother's house. "Just a moment," she said to Hodges, then answered the phone.

"Hi, Renee. Is everything okay?" Mary asked.

"I just wanted you to know that the back screen door on your mom's house is blowing in the wind," Renee said. "It's banging against the siding. You must have forgotten to shut it tightly when you left the house earlier."

Mary frowned. "You saw someone leave the house earlier?"

"Yes. I thought it was you. Wasn't it?" Renee asked, sounding concerned.

"I'll come right over and shut it. Thanks, Renee." Mary hung up and turned to Hodges. "Someone has been in my mom's house again. The neighbor said the person looked like me."

"I'll run over there right now," Hodges said, opening the front door to leave.

"I'm coming with you," Mary said. They both rushed out of the house to Hodges' car.

CHAPTER THIRTEEN

It took them only a minute to drive from Mary's house to Abby's.

"Stay in the car," Detective Hodges said, pulling a pistol out of his glove compartment. "Don't come out until I give the okay."

"Believe me, I'm not going anywhere," Mary said.

Hodges headed to the front door and tried it, then walked around to the back. Mary waited anxiously in the car. This was the second time the back door was left open, even though she knew it was closed and locked. And Renee said she'd seen someone who looked like Mary leaving the house. Who was this person impersonating her, and why were they doing it?

Lights started coming on in the house as Hodges moved from room to room. Mary watched as the lights upstairs came on as well. She secretly prayed he wouldn't find anyone. She didn't want anything bad to happen to him.

Finally, Hodges opened the front door and motioned for Mary to come inside.

"Did you find anyone?" Mary asked when she entered.

"No. Nothing at all. The back door was unlocked again, though. This time, I know it was locked because I locked it for you the last time."

"I haven't been here since that day," Mary said. "This is getting creepy."

"Are you sure no one else has a key to this house?" Hodges asked.

"My Aunt Judy does, but she wouldn't come here late at night. I don't think she's even been in the house since my mom moved to the nursing home. My sister in California has one too, but she's two thousand miles away."

Detective Hodges stared at her for a moment. "You never mentioned a sister before. Is she older or younger?"

"She's five years older and the complete opposite of me. She has blond hair and blue eyes," Mary said. "I didn't mention her because she left home at eighteen and has never been back. She's married with two kids."

"Hm," Hodges said under his breath. "Well, the house is safe now. You should probably look around to see if anything is missing. And you should definitely replace the locks on both doors, just to be safe."

Mary tentatively walked around the first floor. She really didn't want to be in there. Hodges followed her around. In the kitchen, he opened the refrigerator.

"Do you usually keep food in here?" he asked.

Mary shook her head. "Although I can't be sure there wasn't food in the fridge from when my mom was here. I never thought to clean it out."

Hodges frowned. "I don't know. Some of this stuff looks fresh. How long has your mother been in the nursing home?"

"About eight months. She was in the hospital first, then transferred to the nursing home," Mary said.

Hodges closed the refrigerator door. "I think I'll talk to the neighbor to see if I can learn anything else. Would you call her and tell her I'm coming over?"

"Sure. Should I come too?"

"No. It would be better if I just talk to her," Hodges said.

Mary called Renee and said a detective was dropping by to ask her about what she'd seen. After hanging up, Mary looked around the living room, then glanced upstairs. She really didn't want to go up there, but she figured she should, just to see if anything was missing.

Slowly, she walked up the stairs. At the top, she flicked on the light in her bedroom. Everything looked fine. Then she turned on Ginny's bedroom light. It looked the same as before. The bedspread looked like someone had sat on it, but it had looked that way the last time. Snapping off that light, Mary made her way to her mother's bedroom. Quickly, she turned on the light. Everything seemed to be in place. She clicked off the light and hurried downstairs.

At the back of the house, she heard a thump, then footsteps. Hodges came around the corner a moment later.

"How'd it go with Renee?" Mary asked.

"I'm not sure she knew what she saw," Detective Hodges said. "She thought she saw you coming and going from the back door, but then she said she couldn't make out a face or hair color because it was always at night. By the time I was done questioning her, she wasn't even sure if she saw anyone."

"Renee is getting older," Mary said. "And she lives alone. I'm sure any movement or noise scares her."

"Is everything in the house okay?" Hodges asked.

"Seems to be."

"Did you check everywhere?"

"Well, I did on this floor and upstairs," Mary said.

"What about the basement?"

Mary shook her head. "I don't like the basement. And besides, there are only old boxes down there, nothing a burglar would want."

"Why don't you like the basement?" Hodges asked, watching her intently.

"It's where my father died after falling down the stairs. It's just creepy."

"That's right. You told me that before," Hodges said gently. "I'll go down and look around, just to make sure all is well."

Mary followed him to the door in the dining room and watched as he walked down the rickety wooden steps. The only light came from one bulb at the top of the stairs, and then one bulb with a string attached at the bottom. She saw him pull the cord and turn on the light below.

"There's a lot of stuff down here, like you said," he called up. "Say, Mary?"

"Yes."

"Do you normally store your clothes down here?"

Mary frowned. She never even went down there, let alone would put her clothes down there. "No."

"I think you should come down here and look."

Reluctantly, Mary tread carefully down the creaky stairs while holding onto the stone wall. It smelled damp and stale. The basement was full of old boxes, taking up the space her father used to leave open for his workshop. Now, his workbench was cluttered with rusty old tools and boxes. The only open space was where Hodges stood. A broom handle had been placed between two towers of boxes and clothing hung on it.

"Are these yours?" Hodges asked.

At first glance, the baggy suits did look like Mary's clothing. She moved closer and studied the labels on the jackets. Even though her suits were big and baggy, they had been bought from a nice department store and were higher-end labels. These were cheaper versions, but they did look like hers.

"These aren't mine," Mary said. "Mine are from a different store. Plus, the fabric is cheaper."

"Would they have belonged to your mother?"

Mary shook her head. "No. My mom has always been a plus-size woman. These suits are one size smaller than I even wear."

"Then whose clothes are these?" Hodges asked.

Mary thought about the woman she'd seen multiple times following her. The woman's suits looked a lot like Mary's, enough so that she looked like Mary's double. But how could that woman's things get inside her mother's house? Should she tell the detective about the other times she'd seen the woman and show him the texts? But if she did, he might think she was crazy. It would be better if she kept that information to herself.

Mary stepped back. "I don't know, but this is too creepy. I'm going back upstairs." She turned and headed up quickly. The stairs were unfinished with open gaps between each step. Mary moved so fast, her foot caught on one of the boards, and she felt herself falling backwards. She screamed.

"I've got you," Hodges said, standing right behind her. His arms were wrapped around her so she wouldn't fall. "Don't worry. I've got a hold of you."

Mary steadied herself, her heart pounding in her chest. She'd thought for sure she'd end up at the bottom of the stairs, dead, just like her father.

And just like her mother.

She moved slowly up the stairs with Hodges' hand firmly on her waist. It felt good to have someone watching over her. Once they were both upstairs, she closed the door and backed away. "I hate that basement," she said, tears burning in her eyes.

Hodges placed a hand on her back and turned her toward him. He looked down into her eyes, his expression sincere. "I promise. I'm not going to let anything happen to you, okay?"

She nodded as she stared into his bright blue eyes. She wanted so badly to hug him close, but forced herself not to. He was the man trying to solve her ex-husband's murder, not her boyfriend. "Thank you," she said quietly.

They walked toward the front door.

"Something odd is going on around here," Hodges said. "I think the first thing we should do is change the locks on this house. Would you mind if I come over tomorrow afternoon and change them for you?"

"That would be a relief," Mary said. She hated the thought of hiring a locksmith to do it.

He smiled. "Okay. I'll pick them up tonight and meet you here tomorrow in the late afternoon."

"Okay. Just text me when you're ready to come over."

They went outside, and Mary locked the door, even though it didn't do any good. Someone who meant her harm was getting in and out of the house, no matter what she did.

Detective Hodges drove her home and walked her to the front door.

"Thank you for the pizza," Mary said. "And for offering to change the locks."

"You're welcome. I just want to make sure you're safe."

"I know this isn't part of your job," Mary said. "Why are you helping me when I'm a suspect?"

"Like I said. I don't believe that you killed anyone. And it looks like someone is messing with you and trying to pin the murders on you. I'm going to do everything I can to make sure you're safe and solve this case," Hodges said.

"Thank you. I need someone on my side."

"Go on inside and lock the door. I'll call you tomorrow," Hodges said.

"Okay." Mary turned and entered her house, switching on the entryway light. She locked the door behind her, then went inside her living room to look out the window. She watched as Hodges got into his car and drove away.

She was so happy he believed her. Hopefully, nothing else would point the blame at her and she'd lose his trust.

* * *

The next day, Mary slept in since she didn't have to go to the office. Then she showered, dressed, and ate breakfast with Cassie. She wasn't used to having free time on her hands and was unsure of what to do with herself for the next few hours.

Because she was going to meet Detective Hodges later, she decided to call her Aunt Judy and see if they could switch feeding times.

"That will be fine, dear," Judy said after Mary asked her if she'd take care of dinner for her mother. "I hope you have a hot date lined up."

Mary laughed. "Not really. We're going to change the locks on Mom's doors. I think someone has been getting inside the house."

"Oh, that's awful," Judy said. "Well, I'm glad you have someone to help you do that. Better safe than sorry. Say, I saw on the news that your boss was killed in his office. Are you sure it's safe to work there?"

"It was scary," Mary said. "We don't know who did it yet, but I'm sure we'll all be fine there. I'm not going to put in any more late nights, though. I don't like walking outside alone in the evening."

"Keep yourself safe, dear," Judy said.

Mary was relieved her aunt didn't think she had murdered her boss. Hopefully, they'll find the killer soon.

Before going to her mother's nursing home, Mary decided to stop by the mall again and pick out a few more new outfits. She loved her fitted suits so much better than the old baggy ones. And she wanted new jeans and shirts as well. It was nice to finally spend a little money on herself.

She entered the store, and the woman who'd helped her the last time assisted her again. She found several nice suit pieces to mix and match. The saleswoman also suggested a brand of jeans that Mary might like. Mary did like them. They fit perfectly. She bought two pairs, plus some casual tops. She even added a pair of casual wedged shoes to the pile.

"You must have needed a whole new wardrobe," the saleswoman said, smiling.

Mary smiled back. "I did." She stood at the counter, waiting as the woman bagged her clothes. The back of the counter was mirrored, and Mary was absently staring into it.

A woman in a baggy suit with brown hair caught her eye.

Mary blinked to refocus, and there she was. It was the woman who'd been following her. She turned quickly and ran in the woman's direction. Her twin turned and ran too, zigzagging between rows of clothing. Mary ran to the door just seconds after her double had and stopped, looking both ways down the mall. Her double was nowhere to be seen.

Sighing, Mary went back to the counter.

"Are you okay?" the clerk asked, looking startled.

"Did you see that woman? She was wearing a baggy brown suit and looked like me," Mary said.

The saleswoman stared at her. "I didn't see anyone. We're the only ones in the store right now."

"Never mind," Mary mumbled. All the joy of shopping had left her. She paid the woman for her purchases, then left the store. As she walked into the mall, she stopped and looked around her. She knew she'd seen her double in the store. Because if she hadn't, then that would mean she was crazy, and she didn't like the idea of being insane.

Mary walked to her car and stashed the shopping bags in the back seat. As she sat behind the wheel, her phone buzzed. Thinking it was Detective Hodges, she eagerly pulled her phone from her pocket and slid the text open.

"Nice clothes you bought today. I may need to get a whole new wardrobe, too."

Mary sat very still. She had seen someone following her. But who? She looked up and scanned the parking lot. Two aisles away, she watched a black Ford Escape turn down the aisle toward the exit. The person inside waved.

* * *

After her run-in at the mall, Mary wasn't in the mood to help her mom, but she had no other choice. She waved at the receptionist on her way to her mother's room. It was noon, and hopefully her mother's meal had been delivered.

"Hi, Mom," Mary called out when she entered her mother's room. "I switched with Judy today. She'll be feeding you dinner instead of lunch." She looked over and saw her mother lying in bed, her eyes on the television.

Mary walked closer and saw what was on the TV. It was the local news, and they were talking about Mr. Kerrigan's murder. Quickly, Mary grabbed the remote and changed the channel to a game show. "We don't need any depressing news today," she said cheerfully, even though she didn't feel that way.

When she looked at her mother, Abby stared at her with those dark, hard eyes that always gave Mary the chills.

"Let's see what's for lunch," Mary said, turning to the meal tray. "Oh, look. Your favorite. Mashed potatoes with lots of butter. Looks like peas, too, and apple custard. That smells good."

Ignoring her mother's eyes, Mary placed a pad over Abby in case she spat out food, then moved a chair closer to feed her. But her mother's eyes continued staring accusingly at her.

"Mom. I didn't kill my boss," Mary said bluntly. "I've never hurt anyone. I doubt you can say the same. Come on. Let's eat."

Mary rattled on as she fed her mother small bites of food. She told her about the new clothes she'd purchased and how she was changing the locks on the house doors. As usual, her mother spat out the peas but ate the potatoes and custard.

The day nurse came in as Mary finished. "Oh, hi, Mary," she said, smiling. "I expected Judy to be here."

"She and I switched today," Mary said. "I'm finished, if you want to take the tray. I was just going to wipe her face."

"Okay." The nurse continued to stare at Mary.

"Is something wrong?" Mary asked, feeling annoyed. This woman wasn't going to call her a murderer, too, was she?

"Oh, no," the nurse said. "It's just, I could have sworn I just saw you walking down the hallway to the exit minutes before I came in here. But you were wearing a suit, not jeans."

Mary sighed. Had her double followed her in here? Why? "I've been here for the last half-hour," she told the nurse. "It couldn't have been me."

"Right," the nurse said. "These twelve-hour shifts can really get to you." She laughed. "It must have been someone else."

When Mary left, she rushed to her car and locked it. Her double was starting to get brave, coming to a place at the same time as her. It scared her, not knowing why the woman wanted to follow her and send her creepy messages.

Maybe it was time to let Detective Hodges in on what was happening.

CHAPTER FOURTEEN

Mary went home and made sure all her doors and windows were locked. She hung her new clothes in the closet, trying to forget the day's events and enjoy going through the new outfits. Tomorrow, she'd wear one of her new suits. She'd purchased a red blazer she could wear with a white, short-sleeved sweater underneath and black pants. It wasn't exactly outrageous, but for her, it was daring.

Mary ate a late lunch and fed Cassie an early dinner. Finally, around five, Detective Hodges texted her that he would be at her mother's house in five minutes. Mary put on sneakers and walked to the house instead of driving. It was only a block away, and she could use the exercise.

They both arrived at the same time. Hodges wore his dark suit and tie, but he quickly removed the jacket and tie and rolled up his sleeves.

"I bought two new door locks that are strong like a dead-bolt," he told Mary as he pulled a bag out of his car. "They should be harder for someone to break into."

"Let me know what I owe you," Mary told him as they walked up the sidewalk to the house.

"Don't worry about it. I'm happy knowing your mother's house is safe."

Mary unlocked the front door, and they stepped inside. Hodges offered to look around the house first to make sure there were no intruders. After he saw all was safe and secure, he got right down to changing the locks.

"Is there any chance of your mother returning to this house?" Hodges asked as he worked.

Mary sat on the staircase's bottom step. "No. The doctors aren't even offering rehabilitation for her. She's paralyzed from the neck down and has a brain injury."

Hodges grimaced. "Wow. That must have been some fall. And you were the one who found her?"

She nodded her head. "Yes. I was half an hour late coming to help her. I found her at the bottom of the stairs."

"It's a good thing you checked on her each night," Hodges said. He was using an electric screwdriver to unhook the old lock. "Your mother would have died if you hadn't found her."

Mary nodded. Sometimes, she thought her mother would have been better off if she hadn't found her right away. She knew her mother would never have chosen to live like this.

"Can your mother speak?" Hodges asked.

"No. She just stares. But she can swallow, which surprises the doctors. So, that's why I help feed her. I want to make sure she gets enough to eat." Mary watched as Hodges removed the old lock and began putting on the new one. She had wanted to tell him about the woman following her and the creepy messages, but maybe she should wait. It wasn't like it would help him solve the murders if she told him.

"Okay." Hodges stood and handed Mary two keys. "These are for the front door. Let's go work on the back."

Mary followed him to the kitchen and sat on an old counter stool. Her mother's kitchen looked like it belonged in the 1980s, and the appliances were old and scratched up.

"Have you considered selling this house so you don't have to worry about it?" Hodges asked. "Even in its current condition, it would bring in a good amount."

"Conrad kept telling me I should sell it. If I do, the money would go to my mother's care, so I wouldn't make any money off of it anyway. Plus, I'd like my sister to help me clean it out. It will be a big job."

"That's true," he said.

"Are you hungry? I could order take-out, and we could eat dinner when you're finished," Mary asked hopefully. She really enjoyed the detective's company.

"Uh, sure. Or we could go somewhere for a burger. Is there a neighborhood pub around here?"

"Yeah. There's a good one about two blocks from here." Mary was thrilled he wanted to go out. She knew that technically, they couldn't date, but it was fun to have company for dinner.

After changing the back lock and giving Mary that set of keys, they closed up the house, and Mary rode in Hodges' car to the pub. After they entered the cozy, dimly lit bar and found a table, Hodges spoke.

"I have some updates about the case for you."

"Oh." Mary was disappointed. She'd hoped he wanted to spend time with her, but instead, he had business to discuss.

The waitress took their drink and food order and then left. Hodges turned to Mary.

"Your fingerprints weren't found in Kerrigan's office, other than on folders, which would be expected. Unknown prints were found on his desk and on the letter opener used to kill him."

Mary was relieved. "I knew you wouldn't find any evidence from me because I rarely ever went into his office, and I certainly didn't that night. He usually came to my office to yell at me."

"Yeah. Several employees said he wasn't very nice to you. Why was that?" Hodges asked.

Mary shrugged. "I don't honestly know. I always worked hard and never complained when he made me work late to update last-minute files. I figured it was because I was quiet and didn't dress flashy like some of the other women. Who knows?"

"So basically, he was a jerk, and anyone might have wanted to kill him," Hodges said. "Unfortunately, you were in the office when he was killed, and the front camera shows you leaving out the front door."

Mary's eyes grew wide. "So, he was killed while I was there?"

Hodges nodded.

She shivered. "Whoever did it must not have known I was in my office. But I never heard a thing."

The waitress returned with their drinks and food. She smiled warmly at Hodges but ignored Mary when she asked for more napkins.

"The story of my life," Mary said, sighing. "I've always been invisible. Even when I was married to Conrad, women flirted openly with him right in front of me."

Hodges looked at her across the small table. "I don't know why. You're pretty. And you're also smart and interesting, and you have a kind heart."

Mary felt a blush rise to her face. "Thank you. That's nice of you."

Hodges reached across the table and placed a hand on her arm. "I'm not being nice. I'm telling the truth. Obviously, Conrad saw the good in you, or he never would have married you. He was too wrapped up in his own needs to understand you needed to help your mother."

"We were just two very different people," Mary said. "We were compatible at first, but he wanted to have fun, and I had too many responsibilities. I never learned how to have fun. I've always had to take care of someone."

Hodges moved his hand away and lifted his burger. "Well, we're having fun right now. Everyday things, like a meal out, can be fun, too." He smiled.

As they ate, Mary thought again that she should tell him about the woman following her and the texts. But she wasn't sure if that was the right thing to do. She trusted Hodges to help her, yet the messages could also be twisted to make her look guilty. So, she kept silent.

After they'd eaten, Hodges drove Mary back to her house and walked her to the door. "Hopefully, we have your mother's house locked up tightly," he said. "You should be safe when you go there."

"Thank you so much for changing the locks," Mary said. "It definitely wasn't your job to do it, so I appreciate it."

"You're welcome. My job may be to find Conrad's and Kerrigan's murderers, but I need to keep you safe, too. Somehow, you're at the center of all this, and I don't want anything to happen to you."

Mary smiled up at him as he gazed at her with those

gorgeous blue eyes. She wanted him to kiss her, but she knew he wouldn't. His interest in her was because of his job, not as a woman he would get involved with.

"I'll wait until you're safely inside," Hodges said, stepping back.

"See you soon." Mary slipped inside her house and locked the door behind her. She hoped she'd see him soon, but hopefully not because he needed to put handcuffs on her.

* * *

The next day, Mary got ready for work as usual, but she spent more time on her hair and makeup and wore her new red suit jacket, black pants, and white sweater. After feeding Cassie in the kitchen, she poured coffee into her Yeti tumbler and headed out to her car. She'd received a text the night before that the office would be open today, so she was off to work as usual.

"Wow. I love that jacket!" Janice said when Mary arrived at work. "I love how you're sprucing up your wardrobe."

"Thanks." Mary smiled back, feeling more self-assured. She walked into her small office, and her smile faded. Her desk had been torn apart, with the contents lying all over the floor. And her computer was missing.

"Hi, Mary." Roger Clark, one of the two remaining partners, stood in her doorway. Mary liked Roger. He had always been kind to her, and his tall, thin frame and gray hair made him seem less intimidating than Mr. Kerrigan's larger build had.

"Hello, Mr. Clark. I see the police tore my office apart."

"Yes. But they went through the entire office building like a windstorm, so don't feel bad." He hesitated for a moment.

"Would you come into my office for a moment so we can talk?"

"Of course." Mary followed him down the hallway and then across the floor to the front of the building. She figured he wanted to reassign her to one of the remaining partners since Mr. Kerrigan was now gone.

When Mary walked into Mr. Clark's office, she was surprised to see Amanda, the human resource manager there.

"I asked Amanda to join us for our discussion," Mr. Clark said. "Please, sit down."

Mary nodded to Amanda and then sat beside her, opposite Mr. Clark's chair.

"This is difficult, Mary, so please bear with me," Mr. Clark said. "You've been a loyal employee here for twelve years, and we very much appreciate your work. However." He paused.

Mary bit her lip, growing nervous.

"Because of the circumstances of Randall's demise, well, I think it would be better for you to take a leave of absence until the case is settled."

"Why?" Mary asked. "I talked with the detective on the case, and he said I'm not a suspect. They don't know who killed Mr. Kerrigan."

"I'm not saying you were involved," Mr. Clark said quickly. "But, well, your ex-husband was murdered not long ago, and now Randall is dead. It's a big coincidence, and it's making a few of the employees here a little nervous about you working here."

"That's ridiculous," Mary said, anger replacing her nervousness. "I didn't do anything wrong. I've worked hard at my job. I want to stay here."

"As I said," Mr. Clark continued. "It will only be a leave of absence—with pay, of course. As soon as the police clear everything up, we'll be happy to have you return to your current position. Of course, you'll be working with me or Mr. Cunningham, but we can decide that later."

Mary looked from Mr. Clark to Amanda. This was so unfair. They were basically calling her a killer, but in a nice way. "The case could take months. Are you saying you'll keep me on paid leave the entire time?"

"Well, we can revisit it in a few weeks, once more is known," Mr. Clark said. "Please, Mary. It will be best for all concerned. I only have your best interests in mind."

Mary stood. "Fine. But the minute you stop paying me, I'm calling a lawyer. We all know this isn't legal." She turned and left the room, walking straight as a board to her office. She picked up her purse and her tumbler, and when she turned, she gasped.

"Janice! I didn't know you were there," Mary said, her heart pounding.

"What happened? They didn't fire you, did they?" Janice asked, looking concerned.

"Did you want them to?" Mary asked, glaring at her.

"No. Of course not. I wasn't the one who complained. Others said they were uncomfortable with you working here." Janice stood there looking as pretty as ever in a bright pink suit. Mary used to envy Janice, but right now, she was happy she wasn't a back-stabbing bitch like her.

Mary didn't speak because she was afraid of what she might say. Instead, she pushed past Janice and walked out of the office building with as much dignity as she could muster. It wasn't until she was in her car that she allowed the tears to flow.

CHAPTER FIFTEEN

Mary went home and changed into jeans and a T-shirt. If she was going to be unemployed, she might as well be comfortable. She fell onto the sofa, still angry that she'd been told to leave. Cassie jumped into her lap and purred loudly.

"At least you still like me," Mary said, stroking the kitty.

Twelve years. Twelve years of being pushed around by Kerrigan, made to work late because he was so disorganized, and being humiliated in front of everyone else. And what did she get for hanging in there? Nothing. No promotion, and now, no job. All because some woman was impersonating her and showing up at the murder scenes.

"I need to find out who my double is," Mary told Cassie with determination. "And the first thing I should do is visit my twin."

Mary rose and headed to the kitchen counter, where her laptop was plugged in. She sat down and searched for the treatment facility where her twin sister was living. She found it easily and read the rules about visiting a patient. Then, she called to make an appointment.

After three rings, a woman answered the phone.

"Hi," Mary said after the woman had spoken. "I'd like to come there to visit a friend of mine. Her name is Allison Marie Martin."

"Oh." The woman sounded surprised. "Let me transfer you to the assistant director." The phone made a couple of clicks, and then another woman answered.

"I'm told you want to visit Allison Martin," the woman said in a deep, no-nonsense voice. "How are you related to the patient?"

"Ah, I'm not related," Mary said, hesitating. She was, but no one knew about it. "She's an old friend, and her mother said I could contact her."

"I see. Well, I'm afraid Allison Martin is no longer in our facility."

Mary frowned. "What? Her mother told me she was there."

"Yes. I suppose her mother hasn't been informed properly. This wasn't the type of thing we wanted publicity for. Allison Martin escaped the facility nearly a year ago and has yet to be found," the woman said. "I will contact her mother with the information."

Mary froze. Her twin sister, who was in the facility for murdering someone, was loose.

"Ma'am? Did you hear me?" the woman asked.

"Uh, yes. I did. I was just surprised to hear this. Thank you for your time." Mary hung up the phone.

Her twin sister was out there, somewhere.

She had to let Allison's mother know.

Mary searched the contacts on her phone for Colleen's number and address. When she found it, she was about to hit her phone number, then decided against it. It would be better for Mary to speak to Colleen personally.

Grabbing her purse, Mary headed out to her car and drove the twenty minutes to Colleen's home.

She arrived in a nice, older neighborhood of neatly kept homes. Colleen's home was two-stories and had a cottage look. There was a low brick wall in front with a white picket gate to enter the walkway up to the blue door. Flowers bloomed in beds under the front windows, and the house was painted a fresh white. It looked like the perfect spot to grow up in.

She just hoped that Colleen was home.

Mary knocked on the door and waited. She wondered what it would have been like to grow up in this house with Colleen as her mother instead of Abby. Her twin should have grown up to have a normal life, but her genes made that impossible. By a twist of fate—good or bad—Mary could have been the smothered baby brought back to life and grown up here instead. She wondered if living here, with a mother like Colleen, would have made her a more confident person.

No one came to the door, so Mary knocked again. After a couple of minutes, she decided to call Colleen's phone. She stood on the porch as she made the call, and to her surprise, she heard a phone ringing inside the house. Was Colleen home?

A chill swept through Mary. She was sure if Colleen was home, she would answer the door. Hadn't the older woman been the one to offer up her address and phone number?

Stepping off the porch, Mary carefully made her way to the picture window in the front. She tried not to step on the flowers as she moved closer to the window and peered inside. There was a cozy living room with a cream-colored sofa, dark walnut furniture, and a large television on a tall TV cabinet.

She saw no sign of Colleen.

Moving to the right, Mary saw a staircase on the left in the entryway. The further right she walked, the more she saw. Mary gasped! What she saw at the bottom of the staircase made her blood run cold.

Colleen lay on the floor at the foot of the stairs, her head tilted at an unnatural angle.

Panicking, Mary swiped the emergency bar on her phone. She quickly told the operator that a woman was lying on the floor of her home and that she couldn't get inside to help her. As she talked to 911, Mary felt like she was re-living the horror of the day she'd found her mother at the bottom of the stairs. She couldn't believe this was happening again.

Once she'd told the operator the address, Mary hung up and called Detective Hodges.

"Mary. Is everything okay?" he asked when he answered.

Tears filled her eyes. "I'm at a friend's house and I can see her through the window. She's lying lifeless at the bottom of her stairs. I'm so freaked out!" Mary said.

"Did you call 911?" he asked.

"Yes. They're on the way here. I didn't know who else to call." Mary was pacing on the lawn, holding back tears. In the distance, Mary heard sirens coming her way. The next-door neighbor came outside to see what was happening and stared at her.

"I'll be right there," Hodges said. "Give me the address and don't talk to anyone until I'm there."

Mary did, and he hung up. The neighbor lady drew closer.

"Is something the matter?" the elderly lady asked.

Mary turned toward her. "I think Colleen is hurt, or worse. The police are coming."

The woman looked shocked. "Oh, my. I have a key for her door. I'll go get it, so they don't knock the door down." She rushed off and returned with the key as the police and ambulance arrived.

The next few minutes were a blur for Mary. She stayed outside as the police and EMTs entered the house with the key the neighbor had given them. Mary watched as they all shook their heads after examining Colleen. Fresh tears filled her eyes. Colleen was dead. Why was everyone around her dying?

The neighbor lady moved closer to Mary. She was a small woman with silver hair and a kind smile. "I'm so sorry, dear," she said, realizing Colleen was gone. "Aren't you her daughter?"

Mary froze. She turned and looked at the woman. "Uh, no, I'm not. I was a friend of hers. Do you know her daughter, Allison?"

The woman's eyes grew wide. "You look so much like her. I barely know her. I know she's had some medical issues. She's been around here the last few weeks, and I could have sworn you were her."

"You've seen her? Here?" Mary asked, her heart beating wildly.

"Yes," the elderly woman said. "She has brown hair and eyes, like you, and the last time I saw her was yesterday. She was wearing a rather unflattering suit and got into her car."

"Do you remember what type of car she drives?" Mary asked.

"Yes. It's a small black car, like yours over there." The woman pointed to Mary's Ford Escape.

Mary felt like she was going to faint. Her twin, who was capable of murder, was here. And she had to be the person who was following her around.

That meant that Mary was in danger, too.

* * *

By the time Detective Hodges arrived, the EMTs had loaded Colleen's body into the ambulance, and the police were ready to wrap things up. Mary, on the other hand, was a nervous wreck.

"I don't think we need homicide here, Hodges," one of the officers called out to him. "It looked like a simple accident. She must have tripped on her stairs and fallen."

Hodges glanced over at Mary, who sat on the low brick wall.

"Why don't you let me take a look, just to make sure," Hodges said.

The officer nodded. "Have at it," he said.

Hodges walked over to Mary. "Are you okay?"

She nodded, but what she really wanted was to fall into the detective's arms and cry. "Colleen was a nice woman," she said softly. "I just came to talk to her and found her that way."

"Can you wait out here a little longer while I do a walk-through?" he asked.

She nodded again. There was so much she needed to tell him. Now that she knew Allison had been here, she knew Colleen hadn't fallen by accident. She was most definitely murdered.

Hodges disappeared inside the house while Mary waited. She noticed the police officer speaking to the neighbor, and they were both glancing over at her. Mary's nerves tightened. The neighbor probably hadn't believed her when she'd said she wasn't Colleen's daughter. She was probably telling the officer that Mary was lying.

Finally, Hodges strode out of the house, but the police officer intercepted him and talked to him quietly. Hodges nodded, then headed over to Mary.

"We should talk," Hodges told Mary. "I get the feeling that Colleen Martin wasn't living alone in the house."

"I know she wasn't," Mary said. She wanted to blurt out everything she knew right then and there, but she glanced at her watch and saw it was almost time to go to the nursing home. "I want to talk to you, but I have to go take care of my mother first. Can we meet for dinner at six?"

Detective Hodges studied her for a moment. "Yes. Let's do that. But I'll need a statement from you so I can give it to this officer before his shift ends."

"I have so much to tell you. Should I meet you somewhere or at my house?"

"I'll pick you up at your house," he said. "I need to finish up here."

Mary said goodbye and left. If it had been up to her, she would have sat with him immediately and told him everything that had been happening from her first encounter with her twin to Colleen's death. But she had to check on her mother first.

It took thirty minutes for Mary to reach the care facility, so it was a few minutes after five when she arrived. She was impatient to be finished so she could talk to Hodges. When she walked inside, she waved at the receptionist and hurried on her way. As she reached her mother's door, Amy, the night nurse, approached her from the other direction. A crease appeared on Amy's forehead.

"How did you do that?" Amy asked. "I just passed you down the hallway going in the other direction."

"What?"

"You walked right by me just seconds ago. That way." Amy pointed toward the exit door at the end of the hallway. "But you were wearing different clothes." Amy looked confused. "What's going on?"

Mary dashed past her and ran down the hallway, thankful she was wearing sneakers. She reached the door and pushed it open. The cool evening air hit her face as she glanced around. Cars were parked in the side parking lot, but she didn't see anyone walking around.

Had her double been here again?

Panic suddenly filled Mary. Her twin had killed her adopted mother. Had she come here to kill Abby, too?

Running back down the hall, she rushed past a startled Amy and pushed her mother's door open. She nearly fell, making her way into the small room with Amy on her heels. Stopping at her mother's bed, she looked down. Her mother's eyes were staring straight ahead, but something was different about them. They weren't boring into Mary—they were lifeless.

Amy immediately saw the difference, too. She put her stethoscope in her ears and listened to Abby's heart. Then she tried her pulse. "She's gone," Amy said softly, glancing over at Mary.

Mary stared at her mother in disbelief. Gone? Dead? Her mother's face didn't look peaceful. She looked like her last minutes had been horrific.

Her twin had gotten her revenge. Mary knew for certain her twin had suffocated her mother.

CHAPTER SIXTEEN

"I'm so sorry," Amy said to Mary as the two women stood over Abby. "Her heart must have finally given out. Or, she may have choked on something, although no one mentioned she was breathing heavily after lunch."

Mary turned to Amy. Did she really believe her mother had died of natural causes? But then again, at this point, did it matter? "Are you sure the woman you saw looked just like me?"

Amy stared at her strangely. "Yes, she did. She had brown hair and eyes, and her face looked like yours. Except she was wearing a big suit, like you've worn before."

"Did you see her come out of my mother's room?" Mary asked.

"No. I just passed her in the hallway. I said hello, but she kept walking." Amy stared at her. "Who is she?"

Mary shook her head. "I don't know. She's following me everywhere and impersonating me." She glanced over at her mother. "I can't believe my mother's gone. After all these months of living after her terrible fall, it seems strange she'd die so suddenly."

"It happens," Amy said. "But if you don't mind me saying, your mother had no quality of life. She's in a better place now."

Mary knew her mother wasn't in a better place. Abby hadn't been a good person in life, so there was no way she would spend eternity in heaven. She'd suffocated her own baby and pushed her husband down the stairs to his death. Her mother was now in hell.

"Thank you," Mary said, trying to keep her voice steady. "What do we do now?"

Amy explained they'd have the doctor come in and declare Abby deceased, then they could call the mortuary of Mary's choosing to come pick up her body.

Mary told her which place to call, then she hugged Amy. "Thank you for everything you've done for my mother. You've been amazing."

"You're welcome," Amy said. "I'll call for the doctor."

Mary left the room right behind Amy. She didn't want to be in the same room as her deceased mother. She walked out to her car and called the mortuary to start the process, then she called her aunt.

"Hello, dear. Is everything okay?" Judy asked.

"I'm sorry to have to tell you, but my mother passed away this evening," Mary said. "I came to feed her, and she was gone."

"Oh, my goodness!" Judy said. "I'm so sorry. It's so strange. I fed her lunch, and she seemed fine when I left. Do they know what happened?"

"No. Not yet. But considering how bad off she was, the nurse said it wasn't surprising."

"Well, that's true. Wow," Judy said. "We've been taking care of her for so long between the house and the nursing home, it will be strange not to have to do that anymore."

"That's true. It hasn't sunk in yet," Mary said. "Shouldn't I be sad?"

"Oh, honey," Judy said. "I hate to speak badly of the dead, but we both know your mother wasn't very nice to you, no matter how much you helped her. She wasn't nice to me, either, but I knew what she was like when I offered to help. You were a good daughter, dear. No one else would have put up with Abby for that long. Now, you're finally free."

Free, Mary thought. She couldn't understand the concept right now. She'd been catering to her mother for years. It will seem strange to finally be free of that.

"I'll let you know once I figure out the funeral details," Mary told Judy. "I still have to call Ginny and tell her."

"Of course," Judy said. "Take care of yourself, dear. I'll talk to you soon."

Mary sighed when she hung up. So much had happened that day, and she was exhausted. She went back inside the nursing home and spoke with the doctor, then headed for her car. On the drive home, Mary called Ginny.

"Hey, what's up?" Ginny said.

Mary heard music in the background. "Can you talk? Where are you?"

"Oh, I'm at Trevor's recital, but he doesn't play for another ten minutes. What is going on?"

"Mom passed away tonight," Mary said.

"Really?" Ginny sounded stunned. "How?"

"I don't really know," Mary told her. "Aunt Judy said she was fine this afternoon, or at least as fine as Mom could be. But when I arrived at dinnertime, she'd passed."

"Wow. That's incredible! Mary, you're finally free of her!" Ginny said enthusiastically.

"Ginny! That's awful! Our mother just died."

"I know. But let's face it," Ginny said. "She wasn't a nice person, and she used you. Now, you can have your life back."

"That's what Aunt Judy said," Mary told her. "But it's rude to be celebrating that someone is dead."

"Oh, you know what I mean," Ginny said. "I'm not celebrating. Mom wasn't well anyway and would have hated being like that for a long time. You know that."

"That's true. Anyway, I'll have to let the mortuary know what our plans are. Can you come home for the funeral?"

"Oh. Well, honestly, Mary, there's no way I can come there in the next couple of weeks. But if you give me a little time, I can come and we can bury Mom and clean out the house all at once," Ginny said. "Why don't you cremate Mom, so we don't have to have a funeral right away?"

"We didn't cremate Dad," Mary said. "Shouldn't we bury Mom the usual way?"

"Honestly, Mary. Do you think Dad even wants Mom next to him? And does it matter if she's cremated and buried or put in a box? I promise I can come home in two weeks, and we can do everything then."

"Okay. I'll figure it out," Mary said. After all, she was always the one to take care of these things.

"Great. Listen, I have to get back to the recital. I'll talk to you later about when I can come out there. Enjoy your free time. You'll finally have some." Ginny hung up before Mary could respond.

It was almost six o'clock by the time Mary arrived at her house, and Detective Hodges' car was parked there, waiting for her. Her day was far from over.

"I brought Chinese food," Hodges said, lifting a bag up for her to see.

Tears formed in Mary's eyes. After everything that had happened today, she was so happy that Hodges had thought to bring food.

"What's the matter?" he asked as he reached her.

"Let's go inside. I have so much to tell you."

After feeding Cassie and putting out plates so they could dig into the Chinese food, Mary's story tumbled out. She told him about the impersonator who'd been following her for weeks, the creepy text messages, and how she believed that her twin was the person who killed her mother and Colleen. She explained about having a twin who was mentally unstable and harmed people, and how she'd escaped the treatment facility nearly a year ago. Once she had finished speaking, Mary was exhausted. She looked up into Hodges' blue eyes and hoped to see that he believed her.

"This is crazy," Hodges said. "I don't even know where to begin. So, are you saying you think your twin, who you've never met, is behind all these murders?"

"I don't know," Mary said. "All I know is every time some-one was murdered, there was either a video of a woman who looked like me or a witness saying they saw me. But I wasn't in any of those places. So, who else could it be?"

Hodges sat back. "You said you had proof you were born with a twin, and also her death certificate?"

Mary nodded. "Just a minute." She ran to her bedroom and picked up the birth and death certificates, then returned to the kitchen. "Here they are. The attending physician is the one who also signed the new birth certificate stating that Colleen

Martin and her husband were the parents of my twin. They named her Allison Marie Martin. If you look up her birth certificate, you'll see that."

"And you said Allison killed someone and was sent to the treatment facility instead of jail?"

"Yes."

"There should be fingerprints on file for her, then. Maybe even DNA," Hodges said. "But why do you think Allison killed her mother, Colleen? And your mother? Are you sure your mother didn't die of natural causes after months of being injured from her fall?"

"A woman who looked like me was seen moments before I entered my mother's room," Mary said. "It seems obvious to me. My twin got her revenge by suffocating my mother because my mother tried to kill her as a baby."

"What about Colleen?" Hodges asked.

"The neighbor said she'd seen someone who looks like me around Colleen's home for a few weeks. Maybe Colleen let her stay there for a while. If that's true, then she may have pushed Colleen down the stairs," Mary said.

"Hm. It looked like someone was living in the house with Colleen. I saw the guest room bed was messy, and there were clothes around the room. But that doesn't prove it was her daughter living there."

"No, it doesn't. But it's somewhere to start looking," Mary said.

"Wow. Like I said, this is crazy," Hodges said. "Can you show me the texts on your phone again? I need to write the number down and check it out."

Mary gave him her phone, then stood from the counter chair and began putting away their dirty dishes and placing the food in the refrigerator. "I'm exhausted," she said, unable to move another step. She slipped off her sneakers and dropped down on the sofa.

Hodges joined her. "I'll bet you are," he said gently. He lifted his arm up along the back of the sofa as an invitation for her to lie beside him. It felt so good to curl up beside him and lay her head on his shoulder.

"I have a lot of work cut out for me tomorrow," Hodges said. Then he smiled down at her.

"I can't stand the idea of being alone tonight," Mary told him. She had never been forward with a man in her life. Even with Conrad, she'd always let him take the lead. But tonight, she needed to know someone was there to protect her from all the chaos in her life. "Will you stay?" she asked.

He placed a kiss on the top of her head. "I'll stay, but only if you call me Ryan."

"It's a deal." Mary curled in closer, feeling completely safe for the first time in weeks.

CHAPTER SEVENTEEN

The next morning, Hodges was up early and on his way to work, but not before kissing Mary softly on the forehead. He and Mary had moved to her bedroom and cuddled underneath the covers, but that was all. And that was all that Mary wanted. She was falling hard for Ryan, but she wanted to take things slow.

At least until she could prove she wasn't a murderer.

Mary showered and dressed, then fed Cassie breakfast. She had a million things to do, and no one was around to help her. She supposed she could ask her Aunt Judy to help her plan her mother's funeral, but she didn't want to bother her. Her aunt was also now free from caring for Abby, and Mary wanted her to enjoy her newfound freedom.

After eating breakfast, Mary drove to the mortuary. She requested that her mother be cremated, then asked if they could store the ashes until she decided on a date for the funeral. The last thing Mary wanted was her mother's ashes sitting around the house.

After that, she decided it was time to pack up her mother's house. There was no reason to keep it now that her mother was gone. And Mary knew if she didn't start the process now, they'd never finish it when Ginny finally came home. She hadn't seen her older sister in years, but knew Ginny was great at procrastinating, and she probably hadn't changed.

She stopped at a couple of stores and asked for used boxes, and they happily gave her as many as she wanted. Then she bought a box of large garbage bags and packing tape and drove to her mother's house.

As she parked in front of the house, it surprised her that she was no longer scared of going inside alone. Ryan had changed the locks, so she now felt safe. Even if someone had been squatting in the house, they'd be unable to get in there now.

Pulling a pile of boxes out of the back of her car, Mary carried them to the front door. She unlocked it and stepped inside. Dropping the boxes in the entryway, Mary looked around. Everything looked exactly as it had the last time she was here. She thought for a moment, then decided to start in the bedrooms. She'd pack up the things in her room and work her way down the hallway to her mother's room.

Packing up her childhood bedroom felt strange, but was also fun. When she'd moved out to go to college, she'd left so many of her possessions behind. Old yearbooks, family photos, and a few beloved stuffed animals reminded her that her younger years weren't all bad. Sure, her mother was harsh, and she'd missed her father immensely after his death, but she had good memories, too.

Mary sorted items by what she wanted to keep and what to give away or toss. She didn't want any of the furniture from the house or anything else, like bedding, towels, and such. She had everything she needed in her own house and didn't want to bring home reminders of her mother.

She was deep into packing up her room when Ryan called.

"Hi," she said cheerfully. "How are things going?"

"Hi. The DNA reports came back from both Conrad's and Kerrigan's murders," Ryan said seriously. "And it's kind of strange."

Mary sat on her old bed. "What is it?"

"Well, I was able to get the fingerprints and DNA report from the woman you think is your twin sister," Ryan said. "You two do share many of the same markers in your DNA, so she could be your sister. But the expert said she could also be your cousin or aunt."

"Then it isn't one-hundred percent certain she's my sister?" Mary asked. "But Colleen said she was."

"Yes. But I also received recent photos of her before she escaped the facility. And, well, she doesn't look like you," Ryan said. "Granted, having a mental illness and living in a treatment facility all those years is sure to change your appearance. But her hair is short with a lot of gray in it, and her face is round and puffy. Honestly, Mary, she doesn't look at all like you. Not enough for anyone to say they thought she was you."

"But that doesn't make any sense," Mary said. "Colleen's neighbor said Allison had been around the house over the past few days and looked exactly like me."

"I spoke with the neighbor, too," Ryan said. "She did see someone coming and going, but she was uncertain about what the woman looked like. Frankly, I think she has some confusion issues. Her husband sat in on the interview, and he had to keep reminding her of things she'd said."

"Oh." Mary was surprised. The neighbor had seemed lucid to her.

"People tend to freeze up and backtrack when they talk to the police," Ryan said. "So, she may have seen someone who looked like you but was afraid to say it for certain. We might have to interview her again."

"Okay. But did the DNA from the murder scenes clear me?" Mary asked, growing worried.

"There's an issue with that as well. Allison's fingerprints and DNA weren't found at the murder sites," Ryan said. "But, when compared to yours, the DNA found at Conrad's and Kerrigan's murders had markers similar to your DNA. Again, the specialist said it could be an aunt or a cousin. But it could have been mixed with other DNA at the scene, and that's why it's confusing."

"Aunt or cousin?" Mary said, pondering this. She knew her Aunt Judy wasn't capable of killing anyone, and Judy's children lived far away in different states. "Couldn't it be my twin sister's DNA?"

"I'm sorry, Mary. But so far, there's no proof that Allison Martin is your sister. The paper trail proves she's the daughter of Colleen and Adam Martin. We could do DNA on Colleen, but that will take a while to get back. And there's another thing," Ryan said.

"What?"

"I spoke to the hospital administration about Colleen, and they said that they loved having her volunteer, but there were times when she exaggerated stories for attention. She missed working as a nurse and being important. So, if that were true, maybe Colleen told you that story about your twin to feel like she was part of something big."

Mary was aghast. "That's a huge lie to make up just for attention."

"I agree," Ryan said gently. "But sometimes people don't understand that their lies can hurt other people."

"She wasn't lying," Mary insisted. "I know she wasn't. Someone has been following me, and I did have a twin sister. You said earlier that Allison's DNA was close to my own."

"It's not always exact, though," Ryan said.

"But she is my sister!" Mary insisted, on the verge of tears. "I believe Colleen's story."

Ryan sighed. "There's still a lot of evidence to go through. And I'm trying to find more information about the phone that's been texting you. It was activated in Minneapolis, but that's all we know. I need to dig deeper."

"Am I still the main suspect?" Mary asked, her anger slowly turning to fear.

"I'm looking at every piece of evidence to prove you aren't a suspect," Ryan said.

"Will you come over again tonight?" she asked, her voice small. "So, I won't be alone?"

There was a long pause. "I'd like to, Mary. I really would. But I need to work on this case and study all the evidence. I have to figure this out so I can clear your name."

Mary's heart dropped. She knew he was trying to help her, but he also couldn't be with her if she were suspected of murder. "I didn't kill anyone," she said softly. "Please believe me."

"That's what I'm trying hard to prove, Mary," he said gently. "If I learn anything new, I'll let you know."

After they hung up, Mary felt defeated. She'd been so intent on cleaning out the house and moving forward. But now, she just wanted to go home and hide.

She forced herself to work longer at the house because she knew it had to be done. By late afternoon, Mary had cleaned out her room and bagged or boxed everything. She left the stuff she would give away or throw away and put the boxes of things she wanted to keep in the back of her car. Then, she drove home.

Cassie was happy to see her home earlier than usual. Mary unloaded her car and placed the boxes in the spare bedroom. She'd unpack them later. Then she fed Cassie and sat down with a frozen meal for herself.

It felt odd not having to run to the nursing home to help her mother. She'd been doing it for so long that it had become a major part of her life. Now, she had extra time, but didn't know what to do with herself.

As she thought of what Ryan had told her about the DNA matches, she finally grabbed a piece of paper and a pen and started working on a chart. She wrote her mother's name, then hers, then Allison's. She also listed Aunt Judy and Ginny, even though Ginny hadn't lived in Minnesota for years.

If Allison's DNA was close to hers, they had to be related. But Allison's DNA didn't match the DNA at the crime scenes, yet the crime scene DNA matched Mary's a little, enough to possibly be an aunt or cousin. But who could that be? Unless Mary had a relative she wasn't aware of.

No. The person who committed the murders must have been her twin, Allison. There were no other choices. Allison was known to be violent. Maybe the DNA had been compromised. She had to find a way to prove that Allison was guilty.

Mary had an idea. She would park near Colleen's house and wait to see if someone showed up there. Allison wouldn't have anywhere else to go if she'd been staying at Colleen's house. It was worth a try.

"I'll be home later," Mary told Cassie. She grabbed a cloth shopping bag and placed a couple of water bottles and snacks inside it, then ran to her room to find her DSLR camera. It had a super zoom lens she could use to see around the house. Then she got into her Escape and drove the twenty minutes to Colleen's neighborhood.

The sun was just going down when Mary arrived, and she circled the block trying to find a good place to park and view the home. Finally, she parked across the street and one house over from Colleen's house. That way, she could see if anyone entered the front or back yard. Since the house had a connected garage, it would be easy to see someone park in the driveway. She doubted that Allison would be so brazen as to drive right into the garage, knowing the neighbor was watching the house.

Mary took out a water bottle and put it in her cup holder. Then, she picked up her camera and scanned the neighborhood with the zoom lens. There was no alley behind Colleen's house, so unless Allison walked through the neighbors' backyards, it would be hard to sneak in the back way without being seen.

Mary was watching the house intently for almost an hour when a loud rap hit the passenger window. She jumped, her heart beating wildly. When she turned, she saw Ryan's face staring back at her.

Mary took a deep breath to calm herself down and unlocked the doors. Ryan slipped inside, his face creased with anger.

"What do you think you're doing?" Ryan asked, staring hard at her. "You have no business being here."

"How did you know I was here?" Mary asked.

Ryan sighed. "Because we have officers watching the house in case someone goes inside. And, because you have a tail."

"What?" Mary was shocked. "You're tailing me?"

"I'm not tailing you. Another car is tailing you. The officers called me when you stopped here and parked. They didn't want to scare you by approaching the car," Ryan said.

Mary stared at Ryan, completely stunned. "Why are the police tailing me? I haven't done anything wrong."

"Mary. Whether you like it or not, you're a suspect in these murders. And believe me, behavior like this isn't helping you. What did you think you'd accomplish?"

Hot tears filled her eyes and threatened to spill down her cheeks. She knew she was a suspect, but to have someone tailing her was too much. She hadn't killed anyone. She was being set up. "I wanted to see if Allison returned to the house," she said softly.

"And what would you have done if she had? Approach her? Dammit, Mary! We know Allison's a murderer and mentally unstable. Do you think it would end well for you if you got near her?" Ryan looked frustrated.

"I'm sorry. I wasn't thinking. I should have realized the police would be watching the house. I just want all this to be over with." Her tears streamed down her face, and Mary swiped them away with the back of her hand. She felt stupid for not thinking her plan through. Ryan was right. Allison could just as easily have killed her.

"I'm sorry I yelled at you," Ryan said, his voice softer. "But I don't want you putting yourself in danger. I promise. I'm working on this case night and day. I will clear your name, but you have to trust me and let me do my job."

Mary nodded, wiping her tears again. "I'm sorry. You're right. I'll go home."

He reached out and tilted her chin up so her eyes looked

into his. "I promise this will be over soon. Just be patient, okay?"

Mary nodded.

"I'll follow you home to make sure you get there safely," he said, reaching for the door handle.

"You don't have to do that. You said a car is already following me. They'll make sure I get home safe," Mary said.

"Right." Ryan stepped out of her car. "Please go straight home. I'll talk to you tomorrow."

Mary nodded, then put her car into gear and slowly drove away. As she looked up in her rear-view mirror, she saw a set of headlights directly behind her.

When she stopped at a stop sign, her phone buzzed. Mary figured it was a text from Ryan trying to reassure her again. She quickly lifted her phone from the cup holder and swiped at the message.

"Your boyfriend will never figure out the truth."

Mary dropped the phone on the passenger seat as chills ran up her spine. Whoever was texting the messages to her was still following her. It didn't matter how many police officers were watching over her. Mary wasn't safe.

CHAPTER EIGHTEEN

Mary spent a restless night getting very little sleep. The message from her stalker had unnerved her. How did she know where Mary was every minute of the day? And why didn't Mary see the person stalking her except in mirrors or out windows?

She wished Ryan had spent the night. Even if he'd slept on the sofa, she'd feel safer.

The next morning, Mary showered, hoping the hot water would wake her up. She was exhausted, but she had to keep moving. She ate breakfast with Cassie, then packed a lunch. Even though she was tired, Mary was determined to keep working at her mother's house so it would be cleaned out and ready to sell.

Driving her car down the block to her mother's house, Mary noticed an unmarked car following her, then parked across the street from her mother's house. Even though it irritated her that she was considered a suspect, she felt safer knowing the police were watching her. If someone came after her, hopefully, the police could help her.

Carrying empty boxes into the house, Mary set them down and then placed her purse and lunch bag in the kitchen. She grabbed a bottle of water and headed up the stairs with boxes to start cleaning out Ginny's room.

As she went through her sister's belongings, it was hard to know what to keep and what to get rid of. She wished Ginny were here, but she knew that Ginny wouldn't be much help anyway. If Ginny actually came for the funeral, Mary figured she'd head home as fast as she could to be with her family. She wouldn't blame her, either. Mary wished she had a family to go home to every night.

She packed the boxes with Ginny's yearbooks and photo albums and a few knick-knacks that she thought Ginny might like to have. Ginny hadn't enjoyed high school and wasn't involved in any activities. Even though she'd been a pretty girl, she'd never been popular, and having a mom who wouldn't let them bring friends home didn't help either her or Mary socially. They'd learned to become loners, something Mary wouldn't wish on anyone.

It was noon by the time Mary finished with most of Ginny's room. She folded the bedspread and sheets and piled them nicely in a garbage bag. She'd donate all the bedding and towels to Goodwill. Hopefully, someone would be able to use them.

Growing hungry, Mary went downstairs to eat her lunch. She walked into the kitchen, then stopped suddenly. The back door was open. Her heart pounded as fear ran through her. Mary knew the door had been closed when she'd placed her purse and bag in there earlier. She grabbed her purse and ran out the front door. Mary pulled her phone from her pocket and called Ryan.

"Mary. Is everything okay?" he asked, concern in his voice.

"I'm at my mother's house. Someone is in there. They left the back door open," Mary said, still panicking.

"Get out of the house!" Ryan said.

"I already went out the front door."

"Good. Wave the officers over, and they'll search the house. I'll be there as fast as I can," Ryan said, then hung up.

Mary turned to the officers sitting in the car across the street, but before she could wave them over, they were already getting out of their car and heading toward her. Apparently, her fearful expression said it all.

"What happened?" the older of the two plain-clothes officers asked.

"I think someone is in the house. The back door was locked when I went inside this morning, but it was open when I came downstairs just now," Mary told them.

Both men nodded and hurried into the house, pulling their guns from their holsters. Mary waited outside, and that was where Ryan found her a few minutes later.

"Are you okay?" Ryan asked.

Mary wanted nothing more than to fall into Ryan's arms. The past few days had so unnerved her, she felt like she was coming unglued. But she refrained from doing so because she wasn't sure where she stood with Ryan. "I'm fine," was all she said.

"How could anyone get the new keys?" Ryan asked, frowning as he stared at the house.

"I don't know. I haven't even given a copy to my aunt yet. Whoever is getting into the house is determined to scare me." She opened her phone to the latest text message and showed it to him. "I got this last night after you found me at Colleen's house."

Ryan stared at it, keeping his expression neutral. "After they clear the house, we need to talk," he said.

A minute later, the officers came outside. "All clear," the older officer said. "We checked everywhere, but the person must have already left. We closed the back door and locked it."

"Thank you," Ryan said. "I'll be here for a while, so why don't you guys go on a lunch break?"

"Are you sure?" The older officer glanced from Mary to Ryan. "We're supposed to stay close."

"It's fine. Go ahead."

"Okay." They headed to their car and soon drove away.

"Let's go inside to talk," Ryan said.

Mary followed him inside. Ryan closed the door behind him, and Mary set her purse on the staircase's bottom step.

"What do you want to talk about?" she asked, crossing her arms in front of her. Ryan looked so serious that she felt nervous.

"About those texts," he said, handing her phone back. "We were able to trace where the phone was purchased. It was from a Walmart store in Bloomington."

"Really? That's not too far away. Do you think Allison bought it there?" Mary asked, suddenly excited.

"No, Mary." He looked her straight in the eyes. "We found the purchase for it on your credit card. You bought the phone, Mary. You're the one sending those texts to your phone."

Mary's eyes widened. "What? No! I never bought that phone. Someone must have used my credit card number."

Ryan shook his head. "No. It was you. We have you on video buying the phone."

"How? I've never even been in a Walmart in Bloomington." Mary thought for a moment. "It had to be my twin. She must have stolen my credit card and bought it."

Ryan sighed. "Mary. It was you. I can prove it. Call the number from your phone."

Mary looked down at the iPhone in her hand. She went to the texts, then hit the information button. As her finger hovered over the phone number, she looked up at Ryan. "It isn't me. I didn't buy that phone."

"Call it," he insisted.

She touched the number. After a moment, a phone rang inside the house. It was muffled, but it was definitely inside the house. "The person who owns the phone is here," she said, fear rising inside her.

Ryan shook his head. "Look inside your purse, Mary."

"No. It's not in my purse. I'd know if I bought a burner phone, for heaven's sake," she yelled.

Ryan reached for her purse and opened it. He pushed it toward Mary. Reluctantly, she reached inside and pulled out a small, black flip phone that was ringing. She shook her head vehemently.

"I didn't buy this phone. Someone put it in my purse," Mary insisted. "You have to believe me. Why would I send myself creepy messages? It makes no sense."

"My guess is you wanted people to believe that someone was following and terrorizing you. You wanted me to believe that," Ryan said, his eyes sad as he stared at her. "You even went out of your way to be seen on video cameras so you could say it was someone dressing up as you and following you."

"No. Ryan. You know me. I would never do that," she said, desperation in her voice. "I saw someone following me. Did you talk to the nurses at the nursing home? They saw someone dressed like me lurking around seconds before I came in. They saw her!"

"I'm sorry, Mary. I've talked to everyone and watched the footage a thousand times. I combed over all the evidence. But it all points to you. You made it all up, so I'd believe someone was setting you up. And I did believe you, for a time. But the evidence doesn't lie. You killed Conrad so you wouldn't owe him money anymore, and you killed your boss, Kerrigan, because he wouldn't give you a promotion. Then you conjured up the rest to make it look like someone else was the murderer." Ryan sighed. "I have no idea what happened to Colleen Martin, or if you killed her, but I know you killed the other two. And for all I know, you pushed your mother down the staircase as well."

Mary stared at Ryan in total disbelief. How could he accuse her of all those awful things? Backing up, she dropped onto the stairs. "I didn't do any of those things," she said, shaking her head. "And I did see someone following me. I didn't make it up."

Ryan took a step forward. "I believe you truly think someone was following you. But it was all in your head. Mary, I think you need professional help. You lived so long being treated badly by your mother that I think something inside you snapped. But we can get you the help you need. I'll make sure you get a good lawyer and the best medical help."

She looked up at him, aghast at what he'd said. "I'm not mentally ill," she said. "I didn't do those things."

Ryan looked down at her with pain in his eyes. "I'm sorry, Mary. I really am. But I have to take you in."

Tears filled Mary's eyes, and she dropped her head into her hands.

Suddenly, an ear-deafening noise pierced the silence.

Mary's head popped up. Ryan was lying on his back, a bullet hole in his chest.

CHAPTER NINETEEN

"Ryan!" Mary jumped up and went to him, kneeling on the floor beside him. "Ryan!"

"Your boyfriend is dead, Mary," a female voice said behind her. "And he deserved it."

Mary stood and turned. A woman a little shorter than her was standing there, wearing a baggy brown suit and holding a pistol at her side. Her twin. Fear enveloped her.

"Allison?" Mary asked, staring at her twin.

"Mary. It's me," the woman said. "Look at me! It's me!" When Mary didn't respond, the woman pulled off the brown wig to show light blond hair.

"Ginny?" Mary was stunned. "You were the one following me all this time?"

"Yes," Ginny said. "But I was helping you."

"Helping me? How? You shot Ryan!" Mary yelled. "Why?"

Her sister Ginny looked down at Ryan's unmoving form and then back at Mary. "He was going to arrest you for murder, Mary. I had to step in, or else everything I did to help you would be for nothing."

Mary was completely confused. "You murdered people to help me?"

"We don't have time for this right now," Ginny said. "Those cops will be back soon. We need to leave."

"No!" Mary turned back to Ryan. "I have to call 911. I have to help him!"

Ginny grabbed Mary's arm and pulled her back. "He's gone, Mary. You need to come with me or else you'll be blamed for this murder, too."

"I didn't kill anyone," Mary said angrily. "You did! I need to get help for Ryan." She lifted the phone in her hand and realized she was still holding the burner phone. Her eyes went back to Ginny. "Why were you terrorizing me? And why did you put this phone in my purse to make me look guilty?"

"I wasn't terrorizing you," Ginny said, looking insulted. "I texted you, yes, because I wanted you to know that I was helping you."

"Helping me? I never wanted Conrad dead. I didn't want my boss killed, either. And what about poor Colleen Martin? Did you push her down the staircase? Why?" Mary asked.

"Conrad was making you pay for half of the house, and that wasn't fair," Ginny said angrily. "Even you complained about it to me. And your boss? He was a jerk. He never gave you a promotion, and he was cruel to you. I was in your office one morning when I knew you'd be late, and the idiot just walked up to me and started yelling at me to get some files done. He thought I was you. He deserved to die."

Mary couldn't believe what she was hearing. "Wait a minute. I've been calling you, and you were in California with your kids. How long have you been here?"

Ginny dropped her head. "I was here all along. I came back almost a year ago."

"Why did you lie to me? What about your husband and kids?" Mary asked.

"I don't have a husband or kids," Ginny said. "I lied about everything. If you'd known the truth about my life in California, you would have disowned me. I was a failure."

Mary moved closer to Ginny, the gun forgotten. "I never would have done that. What happened? Why did you lie?"

"I hated my life there," Ginny said with disgust. "I couldn't support myself with a real job, so I became an escort. And that's exactly what you think it is. I was paid by high-end clients to have sex. I was so embarrassed that I made up my husband and family." Her eyes brightened. "But then you divorced Conrad, and I decided I could help you. I could start over again, especially if Mom was out of the way. We could sell her house, and you'd get the insurance money from Conrad. We could be a family again."

Mary frowned. "Wait? You came here a year ago?" She clasped her hand over her mouth when realization hit her. "Did you push Mom down the stairs?"

Ginny's pretty face tightened. "She deserved it. You were late coming to help her that night, and she thought I was you. She was yelling at me and saying how useless I was. I just kept thinking that you had to put up with this day after day, and she ruined your marriage. So, when she reached the top of the stairs and stood up, I pushed her. But she didn't die right away, and you showed up right after her fall and called for help."

"Ginny." Mary was appalled. She wondered how her sister could be so cold. "I never wanted Mom to die. She was mean, yes. But no one deserves to die that way." A thought hit her.

"Were you the one who killed her in the nursing home?"

Ginny's face showed surprise. "No. I never went there. I figured time would take care of her."

"Someone was there impersonating me. I could have sworn someone suffocated her," Mary said.

Ginny crossed her arms. "It wasn't me. Listen, we have to get out of here. Now!"

Mary shook her head. "No. You have to get out of here. Take that gun, too. I need to call for help."

"They'll blame you for Ryan's death," Ginny said. "This was Dad's pistol. It's registered in his name. They'll think you found it and shot Ryan."

Mary shook her head. "No. I won't leave him here. Don't you get it, Ginny? I'm falling in love with Ryan. I'm going to do whatever I can to help him." Mary moved to the staircase to pick up her iPhone.

"Don't move!" a man's voice said from behind her.

Mary froze. She looked up at Ginny and saw a look of horror on her face.

"You were dead," Ginny said, her voice shaking.

"No. I was knocked out for a moment, but I'm very much alive, thanks to my Kevlar vest. And I heard everything."

Mary turned. Ryan was standing up, his pistol trained on Ginny. "You're okay," she said, tears filling her eyes. "I thought she killed you."

"Move away, Mary," Ryan said steadily. "I don't want you to get hurt."

Mary took a step back, then saw that Ginny had raised her gun, too.

"You can shoot me, Detective," Ginny said. "But I'll get a shot off too, and this time I'll aim for the head."

"Ginny! Don't!" Mary yelled. "Please. It's over. Drop the gun!"

"Sorry, little sis. But I'm not going to prison," Ginny said. "What I did, I did to help you. To make your life easier. Because I wasn't here for you all those years like I should have been. But I won't be sent away for getting rid of the people who made you miserable."

"I won't let you kill Ryan," Mary said. She'd never felt this determined in her life. Taking a step, she slipped between Ryan and Ginny.

"Mary, don't!" Ryan said. "She'll shoot you."

Mary shook her head. "No, she won't. Ginny, if you really want to help me, you'll put down that gun and give up. I'll do everything I can to help you out of this mess, but I won't let you ruin my life by killing Ryan."

Ginny laughed. "You're the insane one in the family if you think I'll give myself up."

"Please, Ginny. I don't want anything to happen to you," Mary pleaded. "And I don't want you to kill any more people."

Ginny slowly shook her head. "I love you, Mary. I hope you believe me when I say that." She dropped her arm and let the pistol fall to the floor. But before Ryan could react, Ginny lunged forward and pushed Mary into him. Then she ran to the back door.

It took Mary and Ryan a moment to get up off the floor, but Ryan didn't move to run after Ginny. A moment later, the older officer who'd been tailing Mary walked into the room with Ginny in front of him, her arms cuffed behind her.

Mary's mouth dropped open, and she turned and looked at Ryan.

"While you two were talking, I quickly texted the officers

to come back and guard the front and back doors," Ryan explained. "Luckily, your sister didn't shoot me or you."

Mary turned to Ginny. "I'm sorry everything turned out this way. If only you'd come to me first, everyone would still be alive."

Ginny shrugged. "I'm not sorry. I did what had to be done."

The officer moved Ginny forward out the front door to the waiting patrol car.

Mary turned to Ryan. "I'm glad you aren't dead."

He smiled. "I am, too."

"Were you really going to arrest me for the murders before Ginny came along?" Mary needed to know.

His smile faded. "All the evidence pointed to you. I'm sorry. But I'm so happy it wasn't you."

Mary nodded. She didn't know what the future held for her, but she was thankful she wouldn't be spending the rest of her life in prison for murder.

CHAPTER TWENTY

One Year Later
Mary

Mary walked out of the guest bedroom she now used as an office and into the kitchen. Cassie came running, hoping for some lunch. Now that Mary worked from home, Cassie thought she'd be fed every time Mary left her office. She headed to the refrigerator and pulled out leftovers to heat up for lunch. If Cassie was lucky, maybe she'd share a few pieces of chicken from the pasta with her.

After Mary had been cleared of the murders of Conrad and Mr. Kerrigan, she'd been offered her job back at the accounting firm. But after the way she'd been treated, she decided she didn't want to work there anymore. She opened her own small accounting and tax firm from her home, and once she started getting clients, she never looked back. She was making a good income and loved being home and setting her own hours.

"Do I smell something good for lunch?" a male voice called out as he walked into the kitchen.

Mary smiled at Ryan. They'd been living together for six months, and he always tried to be home for lunch whenever possible. He no longer worked in Minneapolis. After solving the murders here, he'd been asked to start a homicide division in St. Louis Park, and his services were used by the surrounding area as well. While homicide wasn't as rampant in the suburbs as it was in downtown Minneapolis, there was enough to keep him busy. Plus, he told Mary he loved being able to see her all the time now instead of two or three times a week.

And they even planned to get married soon.

After Ginny was arrested, it had taken Mary a few days to come to terms with the fact that Ryan had suspected her of murder. But he'd explained he'd done everything he could to find a different suspect. Unfortunately, all the evidence pointed to Mary. So, when Ginny appeared, it had all finally made sense. The strange text messages, the suits in the basement of Mary's mother's house, and the weird sightings of a woman who looked like Mary everywhere. It had all been Ginny.

Ginny had explained that she'd dressed like Mary, worn a wig, and even worn brown contact lenses so people would think she was Mary. She hadn't meant it as a way to get Mary into trouble. She wanted to blend in at the places Mary went for easy access. When she'd appeared at Conrad's door, he'd let her in, believing she was bringing him a check. It wasn't until Ginny had raised the hammer to pummel him that he realized he wasn't staring at his ex-wife. Ginny had found that funny. Mary had not. She hated thinking of Conrad's last moments while Ginny watched the life drain out of his body.

Ginny was also the person who kept entering their mother's home. She'd hidden in the basement every time Mary dropped by to check on the house, knowing Mary would never go down there. When the locks were changed, Ginny had broken into Mary's house late at night, grabbed the keys, and had a copy made before returning the keys to Mary. She told Mary that she should be more careful because it wasn't hard to break into her house. That gave Mary chills.

Since Ryan had heard Ginny confess to everything, and because Ginny didn't want to go to prison, she'd agreed to a deal: she'd spend the rest of her life in a maximum-security psychiatric facility instead of going to prison. Mary was relieved that her sister was there instead of in a federal prison. Ginny needed help; that was obvious. She'd inherited her mother's mental issues, which wasn't her fault, although Mary wished her sister had come to her for help first to avoid the mayhem she'd caused.

Mary had sold her mother's house and placed the money in an account so she could send Ginny spending money each month. And she'd also given the life insurance money she'd received from Conrad to charity. She hadn't wanted anyone to accuse her of profiting from his death.

"Are you going to feed the cat my portion?" Ryan asked, dropping a kiss on Mary's head and then grabbing a plate out of the cupboard. Riley, Ryan's Siberian Husky, was right there by his side, waiting for food to drop. Cassie had been indignant at first over sharing the house with a lowly dog. But once the cat figured out the dog was afraid of her, and she ruled the roost, she learned to accept it.

"You'd better hurry before Cassie or Riley get it all," Mary teased.

Mary was happy. Being with Ryan was easy. She loved him dearly, and he treated her like a queen. She didn't remember being this happy while she was married to Conrad, but that could have been because of all the stress her mother had put on her. Unlike her and Conrad, she and Ryan were completely compatible. After years of being miserable and alone, Mary was finally living the life she'd always dreamed of.

The only thing that continued to bother her was not knowing if Colleen Martin's daughter was truly her twin. She'd asked Ryan about having the remains of the baby next to her father's grave exhumed and tested to see if the child was her sister. But Ryan had talked her out of it. The expense wouldn't be worth it, and the county wouldn't pay for it if it wasn't going to solve a case. Colleen's death was determined to be an accident, and Abby's death was from her injuries. As far as the state was concerned, Ginny was guilty of the two murders, so there was no reason to search for a missing twin sister.

But Mary thought differently. Someone had shown up at the nursing home pretending to be her. Ginny swore up and down she'd never gone there. Why would she lie? She already had two deaths and two attempted homicides on her record. One more wouldn't matter.

And who had pushed Colleen Martin to her death? Colleen wasn't a frail woman. She wouldn't have fallen down the stairs on her own. Someone had to have pushed her. And the neighbor had seen someone who looked like Mary around the house. Yet, to this day, no one had found Allison.

"Are you happy that tax season is over?" Ryan asked as he ate the pasta. "That kept you busy."

"Yes," Mary said, sighing. "But I took on another new client today, so I'll be even busier."

"You're going to have to hire someone to help at the rate you're going," Ryan said, laughing. "You can open your own office—Mary Hodges, CPA—and hire lots of underlings you can boss around."

Mary laughed and shook her head. "Never! I never want to be part of a big office again, even if I own it. I like my life just as it is. And I'm not a Hodges yet."

"Soon, though," Ryan said, reaching for her hand. "Very soon."

Mary smiled. Life just couldn't get any better.

CHAPTER TWENTY-ONE

One Year Later
Ginny

"Ginny. You're doing so well in group, sharing your feelings. You're making excellent progress," Nancy Rierson, the resident psychologist, said at the end of the group session.

Ginny smiled and nodded. She put on a docile façade around Nancy so she'd get good reports. A good report turned into privileges, and Ginny enjoyed getting privileges.

After nearly a year in the maximum security psychiatric facility had taught Ginny that if she played the game right, she could live a better life in the restricted setting. But not too good of a game. She didn't want to be diagnosed as "normal." That would mean she was capable of going on trial for the murders she'd committed, and she didn't want that. As long as she could manipulate the psychologist and other doctors here, she'd do okay.

Ginny spent a lot of her time in the facility's library, either volunteering to help other patients—they were never called inmates—or just reading. In her previous life, she'd never been that interested in learning or reading. But now, she had a lot of time on her hands, and she'd found that she loved reading books about history. She even considered enrolling in some college classes available to patients. Not that she was ever getting out of this place to use a college degree, but it would be a way to keep her mind busy so she didn't actually go crazy.

Because even though everyone thought she was insane, she knew she wasn't. She'd been smart enough to make them think she was, though. Ginny had committed the murders with full knowledge that what she did was wrong. But in her mind, it was doing wrong for the right reasons. And that was why she didn't believe she was insane.

As Ginny walked along the narrow hallway to the library— one of her perks for good behavior was the freedom to go places in the facility unescorted—a female orderly motioned to her.

"You have a visitor coming to see you at two," the orderly said. "So be near the visiting station by one forty-five."

"Thank you," Ginny said cheerfully, getting a smile from the orderly. Always be nice, that was Ginny's motto. Nice behavior brings nice things.

Entering the library, Ginny waved to the head librarian and continued to the history section. Many books were off limits to the criminally insane because the doctors who ran the place thought certain books could cause bad behavior. Nothing with violence was allowed, and neither was anything with the slightest suggestion of sex. But those rules didn't bother Ginny. She enjoyed the historical section—both non-fiction and fiction— and most of those stories weren't considered violent. Well, unless you believe stories of the Civil War aren't violent, which they are. But the powers that be hadn't caught on to that yet.

As she studied the rows of books, Ginny wondered who was visiting her today. Mary visited once a month, right on schedule, but she'd already visited this month. Her Aunt Judy came occasionally, and while Ginny was happy to see her, she could tell Judy was uncomfortable. But Ginny couldn't blame her. The whole set-up was like visiting a prison; talking to someone over a phone with a glass partition between them wasn't the most natural thing in the world.

Ginny hoped it was Mary coming. As promised, Mary hadn't abandoned her. She put money in Ginny's miscellaneous account each month and visited her regularly. She also sent her an occasional card, telling her everything happening in her life. Ginny was pleased that Mary was finally in a good relationship and was happy. By killing Conrad and Kerrigan, Ginny was the one who gave her the chance for a better life. And it didn't hurt that their mother was dead, too. Talk about criminally insane. Their mother had been a terrible person who had made their dad miserable as well as both she and Mary. Ginny knew it was her mother who had pushed her father down the basement stairs all those years ago. So, when she pushed her mother down the stairs, it was sweet revenge.

At one forty-three, Ginny stood up, placed the book back onto the shelf, and walked down the hallway to the visitor center. "Who's here to see me?" she asked the guard at the door.

The woman shrugged. "How would I know? I just take you in and pull you out."

The door opened, and the guard told her to go to station five. Ginny made her way there and sat down. They always let the visitor come in after the patient was seated, so she patiently waited.

A moment later, Ginny smiled when she saw Mary walk

in. Mary looked good. She'd lost a little weight and had styled her brown hair very nicely. She wore new jeans, a nice leather blazer, and a pretty pink blouse underneath. Ginny sighed. She missed wearing nice clothes. The patients wore blue scrubs with Crocs, which were comfortable, but she got tired of always wearing baggy clothing.

Mary sat and lifted the receiver on her side. Ginny did the same.

"You look great, Mary," Ginny said, smiling at her sister. She knew the orderlies were always watching their behavior, even when they visited with family.

"Thanks, sis," Mary said, smiling back.

Ginny frowned. Mary never called her sis. "So, what's up? You already visited this month."

"Do I need a reason to visit my big sister?" Mary asked.

Ginny stared at Mary. Something was off. Her eyes were different. Darker. So much like her mother's evil-looking eyes. And when she smiled, her front tooth was crooked. Ginny knew that Mary had paid for Invisalign braces after she'd been working for a few years. Mary's teeth were straight.

"What's wrong, Ginny?" the Mary look-alike asked. "You look confused."

"Allison?" Ginny asked, her voice low. "Is that you?"

The woman laughed. "You're not stupid, that's for sure. I thought it would take you longer to figure it out."

Ginny's heart raced. Mary had been right all along. Her twin was alive. "What are you doing here?"

"Oh, I just wanted to see how you were doing on the inside," Allison said. "You still look good, I guess. But wait until you've been here for a few years. It takes a toll on you, believe me."

Ginny remembered the photo of Allison that Ryan had

been given and how bad she'd looked before breaking out of this very same institution. But now, it looked like she'd lost weight and dyed her hair to match Mary's. If Ginny hadn't known her sister so well, even she would have believed Allison was Mary.

"You'd better stay away from Mary," Ginny said, her tone threatening. "I swear, if you do anything to ruin her life, I'll…"

"You'll what? You're in there, remember? There's nothing you can do," Allison said. "But don't worry your pretty blond head about me. I don't want to hurt Mary. I'm only imitating her, so no one knows it's me. Besides. If it wasn't for me, our crazy mother would still be dragging Mary down, and she probably wouldn't have that cute fiancé."

Ginny frowned. "You? What do you mean?"

Allison moved in closer and spoke quietly. "I finished what you messed up. You may have pushed dear mother down the stairs, but I'm the one who smothered her. Just like she smothered me as a baby. It was sweet revenge."

Ginny's eyes grew wide. "You were the one the nurses saw at the nursing home and thought it was Mary."

"You bet your sweet ass I was," Allison said. "And I got rid of my adoptive mother as well. I mean, I really cared about her, since she saved my life and took me in, but she was the one to have me committed for all those years. And then she blabbed to Mary about my being alive. She just had to go. After all, pushing a loved one down the stairs is in the blood, isn't it?" She laughed again, sounding maniacal.

"You should be in here," Ginny said sharply. "Then everyone would be safe from you."

Allison's face hardened. In that face, Ginny saw pure evil.

"Well, it's been a nice visit, dear," Allison said, her

expression returning to a smile. "You know, Mary's fiancé is awfully handsome. If I get tired of what I'm doing now, I might just decide to take over her life. It's not like he'd know the difference. He actually believed for a time that Mary was the one who murdered those two people. I bet he'd never question it if I got rid of Mary and became her."

"Don't you dare. I swear! If you do anything to Mary, I'll get out of here and kill you!" Ginny yelled.

"Good luck with that. Bye-bye, big sis." Allison hung up the phone and slowly made her way out of the room.

"Get back here! I swear! I'll kill you!" Ginny screamed. The guard entered the room, looking surprised at what Ginny said. "You have to stop her!" Ginny screamed at the guard. "She's going to hurt my sister. She's crazy. She belongs in here! Stop her!"

The guard grabbed hold of Ginny and dragged her out of the room as the other patients with visitors looked on.

Ginny had finally lost it. And no one was ever going to believe that it wasn't Mary who'd visited. It was Mary's evil twin.

-End-

Mary's troubles are not over yet –

Mary, Mary, Book Two, Allison's Revenge,
will release by fall 2025.

ABOUT THE AUTHOR

D. L. Sletten writes domestic thrillers and psychological suspense novels. Sletten lives in Minnesota, plotting books in a cabin in the woods.

Connect with D. L. Sletten at: www.dlsletten.com.